Rebel on a Rock

By the same author

THE SECRET PASSAGE

ON THE RUN

THE WHITE HORSE GANG

A HANDFUL OF THIEVES

THE WITCH'S DAUGHTER

THE RUNAWAY SUMMER

SQUIB

CARRIE'S WAR

THE PEPPERMINT PIG

DEVIL BY THE SEA

Rebel on a Rock

by

NINA BAWDEN

LONDON
VICTOR GOLLANCZ LTD
1978

WY

ISBN 0 575 02420 8

PRINTED IN GREAT BRITAIN
BY EBENEZER BAYLIS AND SON LTD
THE TRINITY PRESS, WORCESTER, AND LONDON

For Austen

A present from Monemvasia

Chapter 1

When I was twelve years old I stopped a war. Not a great war, like World War Two, or Vietnam, but a war all the same: a revolution in a foreign country. My stepfather, Albert Sandwich, says I mustn't tell you the real name of the country, nor the real names of our friends who live there, because if the government should change and a bad one come into power again, they might be thrown into prison and tortured, but the rest of this story is true. It's important to tell the truth in this sort of book, Albert says.

It's hard to know where to begin. "At the beginning, you dope," my brother Charlie says—Clever-Dick-Charlie!—but he can't tell me when that was. Whether it was when I met my friend Alexis and he told me his secret, or earlier, when I thought Albert was being a spy. Or several months before *that*, when Albert married our mother and took us four children on as his family: Alice and James and Charlie and me. It was Albert who took us to Ithaca. We would never have gone there without him.

Albert says not to worry too much. Just to pick the point when I first knew, for myself, there was something strange happening. Albert says, "Write what you remember, Jo, not what I told you."

Albert was always telling us things. He always stopped what he was doing when we asked questions and answered them carefully, even if it was something quite simple the little ones wanted to know, like why they couldn't breathe under water like fishes, or where babies came from. Sometimes his explanations went on too long for them. James went to sleep as he did when he was bored, and Alice stood on her black, woolly head and hummed to herself.

When we knew we were going to Ithaca, Alice asked, "What's it like, Albert?" All she wanted to know was if we were going to the sea for this holiday, and if she could take her inflatable duck, but instead Albert talked about politics. He told her that Ithaca wasn't a free country with an elected government like England or America. It was ruled by a Dictator who put people in prison if they didn't agree with him. "Will he put *me* in prison?" Alice asked hopefully—she was only seven and thought this sounded exciting—but when Albert said, "No, of course not," she lost interest and hung upside down from her chair like a bat and started her humming.

Albert seemed not to notice. He pushed his glasses up on his nose and went calmly on. I could tell he wasn't really speaking to Alice but *through* her, to Charlie, who was lying on the sofa with his eyes closed, pretending to be bored as he often did when Albert was talking, but secretly listening. A mean trick, I thought, and I tried to make up for it. I tried to pay attention to Albert's lecture on Ithaca because I loved him and wanted to please him, but being taught things has always made me feel tired. Especially history . . .

"Leave it out, then," Albert says. "Just write what you thought when we landed in Ithaca. Write as if you were someone else watching us all because that will be easier, but write what *you* saw, what *you* felt. The truth will come out better that way."

"It was hot. My ears hurt. I was angry with Charlie. That's not the *story*."

"It'll do for a start," Albert says.

Charlie said, in the plane, "*Albert says, Albert says*! Why do you keep saying *Albert says*? As if it was Holy Writ?"

Charlie and Jo were sitting towards the front of the cabin and their mother and Albert and the two little ones were at the back, near the toilets, because James was often sick when he travelled. It was clear to Jo, who was an intelligent girl (it is embarrassing to write this but I am trying to be truthful as Albert says I must be) that this was why Charlie was being so snarky. After their father died it had always been Charlie who looked after their mother on journeys, finding her handbag and keys when she couldn't remember where she had put them, minding the tickets and taking James to the toilet. Now she didn't need him to help her because she had Albert for that.

"I only said Albert told me to swallow when we came down to land," Jo said crossly. She had tried to be patient with Charlie ever since they'd left London, letting him have the window seat and putting up with his jealous temper, but now her ears hurt too much. As the aircraft lost height, sinking down through pink, feathery clouds, the pain became sharper, like nails driving in. She rolled her head about, groaning.

"It hasn't worked, has it?" Charlie sounded smug; green eyes bright with malice. "Albert doesn't know everything!"

"Shut up, Charlie. Perhaps I didn't swallow hard enough. Are we down yet?"

"Look." Charlie pulled her across him to look out of the window at the white city appearing beneath them. Blue sea with foam at the edges crawled round three sides of it like a fringed shawl.

"Zenith," Charlie said. "The capital city of Ithaca. Try pinching your nose and blowing."

The plane bumped on the runway. At the edges, brown grass and red poppies blew backwards. Jo's ears popped but didn't clear properly. They seemed clogged with cotton and when she stood up she felt giddy. Giddy going down the steps of the aircraft, white sun stinging her eyeballs, and glad when Charlie took her hand at the bottom even though she was still cross with him. She clung to his hand. She said, "It's so hot. Like an oven. And my ears are still hurting."

"Don't moan," Charlie said.

Heat danced in the air. It was cooler inside the airport building and smelled tangy-clean, like a hospital. Noises echoing from the low roof sounded woolly to Jo. Her ears popped again, louder this time, like a gun going off in her head. She heard her voice ring out, clear at last. "Where are the others?"

"Don't shout," Charlie said.

They were coming towards her, Albert carrying James, fast asleep and slung round his neck like a scarf, and holding Alice with his free hand. His glasses slipped helplessly down on his nose. He said, "We'll have to wait a bit, I'm afraid."

The other passengers were already filing through immigration; a party of tourists laden with cameras and shoulder bags and sun hats and plastic carriers bulging with cartons of cigarettes and bottles of duty free gin. Alice said, "Why should all those other people go first? Before *us*? It's not fair."

She hopped round in circles, jerking Albert's arm about as if it was a lead and she was a badly trained little dog on the end of it. "I don't want to wait! I'm getting bored waiting!"

Albert said, "It won't be for long. All the others are in a group. You can tell by the labels on their hand baggage. You see that man with a cap? He's their courier and he's got all their tickets. Please be good, Alice darling."

"I'm always good," Alice said in a loud, outraged voice. Heads turned in the line at the barrier. And stayed turned.

"Shut up, Alice," Jo said. "Drawing attention. You always do it! Making people stare at us!"

"Why shouldn't they?" Charlie said.

"You know why."

"Do I?" Charlie looked at her, raising one eyebrow and grinning. A mocking, sly grin. Jo breathed deeply to calm herself; to stop herself hitting him. Charlie said, "All right. I suppose I do know, but I think you're just stupid. People only stare because we look interesting. More interesting than most families. You should be pleased, really."

Jo sighed. Charlie was right, she knew he was right, she ought to be proud to be different, but she couldn't help how she felt. It embarrassed her to know how peculiar they must look to strangers. Except Charlie, who was like their mother, thin as a bean pole with eyes like green emeralds, none of them looked as if they belonged. Albert's appearance was odd enough, anyway; his clever, rubbery, squashed-up face almost hidden behind huge, heavy glasses that kept slipping down on his nose. Jo had her father's pale skin and red hair, but since he was dead now, no one could tell she was one of this family, and Alice and James were even more out of place, being adopted, and black. At London Airport, Jo had seen their reflection as they had all walked together towards one of those glass doors that open like magic before you, and, for a second, before she realised who they were, she had thought—*what a funny, mixed lot*!

Even their names were different. Albert Sandwich and his wife, Carrie, and her children whose name wasn't Sandwich but Popper, which had been their father's name. When Albert and Carrie got married, Jo had wanted to change her surname, as her mother was doing, to avoid explanations at the new school she was going to, but Albert had said it would upset Charlie. "It upsets *me*, not changing," Jo said, but for once Albert had paid no attention, and had simply said, very firmly, that it would upset Charlie more. Albert hadn't even asked why she minded, Jo thought now, feeling surprised and resentful, as the tourist group disappeared finally and it was their turn to go through immigration and hand over their passports.

Mr and Mrs Sandwich and the four Popper children, two white and two black. No wonder the immigration officer, a short, sweating man in a tight, uniform jacket, was looking suspiciously at them. Jo felt laughter curling inside her, tickling the back of her throat like a feather and half hoped he would say, "What's all this, then? Have you kidnapped these young ones? They don't belong to you, do they?" But when the man had glanced at their passports, his brown eyes flickered incuriously over their faces—like a darting fly, Jo thought—and landed on Albert's. He said, "Wait. Please. One minute."

He had a box on his desk. A card index. He flipped through the cards with stubby, dark fingers and Jo, standing close, saw that the one he stopped at had Albert's name on it. There was something written beneath it but it wasn't in English.

The man looked at the card and then at the six of them, a long, cold, careful look this time. Chilled by that look, Jo stood very still. She rolled her eyes sideways at Albert and was relieved when he winked at her. Then the man stamped Albert's passport along with the others and pushed them back over the counter.

No one spoke until they were out of the building. Even Alice was quiet, walking on tiptoe, as if she'd been told someone was sleeping. Out in the sun, in the clean, dazzling brightness, Albert said, "It's all right, Jo! Don't look so solemn! They were just checking on me. Once you've been here a few times, they start a file on you. Write down who you are, why you've come, who your friends are. We were lucky today. Last visit, they kept me a couple of hours, asking questions."

Carrie laughed. She was carrying James now and he was struggling awake and starting to whimper and roll his eyes up until the whites showed. "Well, you've given them something to put in your file now, haven't you, Albert? Your new, funny family."

"Why funny?" Jo said. "Why are we funny?"

She glared at her mother and Carrie looked startled. "Well, we are a bit aren't we? I was surprised that man didn't search us all, really. Go through our baggage!"

Albert said, "Ssh, darling," flashing his glasses like indicators in the direction of the taxi drivers who were waiting well within earshot and Carrie laughed again and said, "Albert Spy-Boots," to tease him, but softly, so that the men couldn't hear her.

Alice said, "It's Sly-Boots, not Spy-Boots. If that man had searched me, he'd have found the gum in my knickers."

"You shouldn't chew gum," Albert said. "It ruins your teeth." And waved to a taxi.

The taxi was old and bouncy; springs jangled as it swerved round the corners, the driver blowing his horn. The city of Zenith was full of cars and buses and trucks and taxis, all blowing their horns at one another as if they were carrying on a loud, friendly quarrel. Full of people, too, sitting at pavement cafés, or strolling along, laughing and talking and waving their arms about. A cheerful place, Jo thought, leaning out of the window and enjoying the cool feel of the wind blowing her hair back; a bright, jolly city . . .

They were driving along what seemed the main street, wide and planted with trees, when the driver braked so suddenly that they fell off their seats and a following van bumped into the back of them. They had reached an intersection where the lights were green but a siren was screaming. Apart from the siren, everything seemed to have gone quiet suddenly. No horns blew. At the side of the road, the people who had been talking so merrily a moment before now stood silent and watching.

The siren came closer. "Fire engine," Alice cried eagerly, scrambling up from the floor of the taxi and butting at Jo with her head to get past her and look out of the window.

But it wasn't a fire. The next second, motor bicycles went roaring by, a long, double line of them, ridden by men in black uniforms with hard, white hats on their heads. An army truck followed, soldiers sitting high up, guns over their knees threatening the street either side of them. Then an enormous, black limousine with blinds drawn, flanked by more policemen on motor bikes, then another truck, full of soldiers . . .

Jo looked at Charlie and saw his jaw hanging open. He closed it and swallowed. No one said anything. The siren faded away in the distance. The taxi man got out and went to speak to the van driver behind him. He pointed at the back of his taxi and started shouting excitedly. The rest of the traffic began to move again, but more slowly, and even the shrill horns seemed muted.

Albert turned round from his seat in the front. "That was the Dictator," he said. "You have just seen the Dictator drive by with his bodyguard." He wrinkled his rubbery nose as if he smelled something nasty.

Jo's stomach felt fluttery. Even the Queen didn't drive round London like that, protected by guns and drawn curtains. She said, "What's he scared of? All those police! All those soldiers!"

"He's not scared, dopey," Charlie said. "It's just to show off. Show he's the Boss."

"Partly that," Albert said. "But Jo's right, he's scared, too. Tyrants usually are. The Dictator is afraid of the people and the people are frightened of him. Especially here, in the city. There are Secret Police everywhere, in the streets, in the cafés. Even hotel rooms are bugged, sometimes."

Charlie laughed shortly. Albert looked at him thoughtfully and he flushed and stared out of the window.

Carrie said, "I'll be glad to get out of Zenith."

Her voice sounded shaky. Albert leaned over the back of the seat and touched her knee lightly. "I know, love. I'm sorry. It's just this one night."

"All right," Carrie said. "*I'm* all right. I'm not worried. As long as you're careful."

"You know me," Albert said. "Caution is my middle name."

The children watched them smile at each other. Their smiles seemed to pass a message between them. Charlie looked at Jo, widening his eyes and turning the corners of his mouth down as if to say, "What's the secret?" Jo frowned at him and he shrugged his shoulders accepting that this wasn't a time to ask questions. The driver got back in the taxi, slamming the door angrily, and they were all quiet for the rest of the journey.

When they got to the hotel, everyone came out to meet them; the doormen, the porters, the clerks from reception. They crowded round Albert with welcoming smiles, shaking his hand like old friends. The hotel manager came down the steps, arms outspread. He was a square man with great, thick, short arms like a bear and two gold teeth in the front of his mouth. Gold flashed as he embraced Albert and kissed him, first on one cheek, then on the other. "My wife," Albert said. "My stepchildren."

"You are all welcome," the manager said. "We have good rooms prepared for you. Mr Sandwich is my good friend."

He bowed over Carrie's hand, then, to Jo's embarrassed amazement, took hers. He didn't touch it with his lips but she could feel his warm breath. She was too surprised to speak but Alice pushed past her and said, "How do you do?" sounding very prim and polite. She always had beautiful manners with strangers and she looked beautiful, too, in the scarlet party dress she had insisted on wearing to travel in, and a scarlet bow pinned on her head among her tiny, black pigtails. The manager's eyes opened wide as he bowed to her. He said to Albert, "One would say, a young Princess!" and Alice smiled proudly.

Uniformed men took their suitcases. They went up in the lift to their rooms which were more like rooms in a palace than in a hotel; silk-covered chairs and bowls of flowers everywhere. Two rooms, one for Carrie and Albert and one for the children, with a huge, marble-floored bathroom between them.

When the porters had gone, Carrie said, "It must cost a lot, Albert. Can we afford it?"

He laughed at her worried face. "They are my friends here. Ithaca hospitality is famous, darling. They would be ashamed to do less for us."

He was smiling, but when the telephone rang in the room his face became suddenly serious. He picked it up, pushing his glasses high on his nose and holding them there. He said, "Yes." Then after a pause, "Yes. In half an hour, then."

He put the receiver down; looked at Carrie. She looked back at him. He said, "They're quick off the mark. Can you manage? Best to get it over and done with."

Carrie nodded. She had put James down on the bed. He curled up, thumb in his mouth.

Charlie said sternly, "He won't sleep tonight if you let him sleep now. You know what he's like."

"There's a park behind the hotel, Carrie love," Albert said. "Why don't you take the little ones there? Jo and Charlie can come with me if they want to."

"I'll stay," Charlie said. "I'll stay and help Carrie."

He had called his mother Carrie ever since Dad had died. Most of the time it sounded quite natural—it was her *name* after all!—but the way he said it to Albert now, it sounded more like a challenge. A glove thrown between them. How dare Albert leave Carrie alone in this sinister city full of soldiers and Secret Police, while he went off on some mysterious errand! Albert grinned at him cheerfully. "Perhaps that would be a good idea, Charlie. If you really don't mind. Do you want to wash, Jo?"

"Oh no," she said. "I'm quite ready."

Chapter 2

She would have liked to go to the bathroom first but she was afraid that if she did Charlie would change his mind and decide to come too. It was lovely to have this chance to be with Albert alone, even if, once they had left the hotel, he seemed hardly to notice her, walking so fast she had to run to keep up with him. It was late afternoon, almost evening; the sky was dark blue with lemony streaks above the brown hills to the west of the city, and the streets were crowded and busy. They came to a square full of trees and open-air cafés, all packed with people talking and laughing and shouting to friends who passed by. Jo caught Albert's sleeve. "Everyone seems to know everyone else. Do they ever stop talking?"

"Hardly ever. It's the chief entertainment in Zenith. Would you like an ice-cream?"

They sat on rickety chairs, at a rickety table. Albert ordered a small cup of coffee that looked thick as syrup and a drink in a tall glass that turned cloudy when he added water. Jo's ice was delicious, with bits of nut and dark chocolate. While she ate, she watched Albert. He was wearing the heavy jacket he had put on when they left home that morning.

It had been chilly in London but it was hot now, in Ithaca. There was sweat on his forehead. Jo said, "You must be boiling to death in that coat, why don't you take it off?" He smiled at her vaguely. He had heard her, she thought, but only with his ears, not with his mind. His mind was elsewhere. He was making a little, hoarse, grunting sound in his throat as if he was very pre-occupied. She said, "Are we waiting for someone?"

"Perhaps. Don't look round. Concentrate on your ice. You're enjoying it, aren't you? What's in it?"

"Chocolate and nuts. And something else. Something spicy."

"They're famous for their ice-cream in Zenith," Albert said, speaking loudly and smiling as if he found this conversation most interesting. But he was looking beyond her. Someone was coming—was standing beside them! Jo looked up shyly—Albert had said, *don't look round*, nothing about not looking *up*—and was disappointed to see it was no one important, only a pedlar, selling nuts in small, paper cones.

Albert said, "You should try these nuts, Jo. They're pistachios. We'd better get some for the others too, hadn't we?"

He took four cones and gave one to Jo. He paid the man with a note and fumbled the change, dropping coins on the ground. The pedlar bent to pick them up for him and, as he straightened, his face on a level with Albert's, Jo thought he spoke into his ear. It was over so quickly she couldn't be sure; the pedlar had gone, threading his way through the tables, and Albert was saying, "We ought to get back, I think. Alice and James will be wanting their supper."

Watching him lift his glass to finish his drink, Jo saw his hand tremble. She thought—*Albert's scared*! This scared *her*—then she saw how she could help him. He had brought her with him to make whatever it was he was doing seem casual and ordinary; a kind father taking his daughter to a café for an ice-cream! She scraped her dish clean, rolled her eyes, and said, in a carrying voice, "That was absolutely *super*, Albert. Really *great*, honestly! It was *lovely* of you to take me out for this treat when you really wanted to stay and unpack! Thank you so much."

He looked astonished; eyes wide behind his thick lenses. Then, understanding, he smiled. "Don't mention it, Jo. You're very welcome." As they stood up he took her hand and squeezed it to warn her to say no more now. They walked out of the square, up a steep, narrow street, then along a side alley with tall houses on either side and lines of washing strung between iron balconies. Albert walked fast, not once looking behind him, though Jo sensed that he wanted to. Was he afraid someone was following? She listened for footsteps but heard only their own, echoing in the quiet street. They changed direction, down a flight of stone steps and along another alley that doubled back on their own tracks. "A short cut," Albert said, as they came to a main road with hooting traffic and brightly lit shops. "Seems more like a long one to me," Jo said and Albert laughed.

In the main street, he stopped at a kiosk that sold tobacco

and newspapers and asked for a packet of cigarettes. He took his time paying for them, feeling in his trouser pocket, rejecting the coins he took out and reaching inside his jacket instead for his wallet. People pushed past, jostling them; Jo glanced at faces but no one seemed interested in what Albert was doing. No reason why they should be, she thought—*she* knew Albert didn't smoke, but they didn't. She saw him take a fat envelope out of his pocket along with his wallet and, as he did so, a man appeared beside him, a squat, tubby man in a dark suit, and took it. No words were exchanged. By the time Albert had paid for the cigarettes with a note from his wallet the man had vanished into the crowd.

Albert sighed, a long, hushing sigh. It was as if he had said, "Well, that's over."

Jo didn't dare speak until they were almost back at the hotel, walking through the small park behind it. Albert sighed again, that tired, relieved sigh and sat down on a stone bench as if he felt too weary to go any further. Jo looked around her. It was dark now and the park was empty. There were no bushes near where someone could hide, watching and listening . . .

She said, "Albert. . ." and stopped, feeling foolish. What she had been going to say seemed so ludicrous. But Carrie, her mother, had said it. She had said, "*Albert Spy-Boots.*"

Jo puffed out her cheeks and slapped at them sharply, making a noise like a paper bag bursting. She said, "You're not a spy, Albert, are you?"

She expected him to laugh but he didn't. He kicked at the

gravel with his left foot, stared down at his dusty shoe with a gloomy expression and said, "No, I'm not brave enough. I'm just a postman."

"*A postman?*"

Albert cleared his throat. "Of a sort. That is, I brought in some letters. From old friends of mine who left Ithaca when the Dictator took over, to their friends and their families who are still living here. If the letters went through the mail in the ordinary way, they would be opened and read by the censor."

Jo felt let down. All that dodging about, all that *fuss*!

She said, "Why were you scared then? If that's all you were doing. Just carrying *letters*!"

"Instead of nuclear secrets on micro-film, do you mean? Well, letters can be dangerous, too. It depends what they're about, doesn't it? I've no idea what was in that lot I had to deliver, but I don't imagine they were all birthday greetings. It might have been rather uncomfortable if I'd been caught with them on me. Not so much for me as for the people they were addressed to. None of my friends are exactly in favour here, just at the moment. But I must admit I was scared for myself! I'm not brave, as I said." He sounded quite cheerful as if he wasn't ashamed to admit this. "Not like your mother."

"Mum's not brave," Jo said. "She's a terrible worrier."

"That doesn't mean she's not brave. She might worry, but if she thought something was the right thing to do, she'd go on and do it, even if it was dangerous."

"You would, too," Jo said. "I mean, you did *now*. Being a postman. It's even braver, in a way, to do something that scares you."

Albert got up and bowed. "Thank you for those kind words, Miss Popper. You make me feel like a hero."

"Don't laugh at me."

"I'm not laughing." He took hold of her hands and pulled her up and kissed her forehead gently. "I was just being silly because I was glad it was all finished with. Mission accomplished—and thank you for helping me. You did pretty well in the café."

"I over-acted. Anyone watching would have guessed something was up."

"Only if they knew you weren't usually quite so effusive. Lots of girls talk like that."

"Silly girls."

"Yes. You're not silly."

"Thank you." Jo was suddenly hungry for compliments. "Would you say I was grown up for my age?"

"I think you are, very probably."

"As grown up as Charlie?"

"Almost."

"Only almost?"

"Well." Albert hesitated. "He's fourteen. Two years older than you. And he's had a lot of responsibility."

Jo looked up at him. His face was a pale blur above her. It was easy to talk in the darkness. She said, "I could have helped Mum more if she'd let me. But she only let Charlie, she didn't want *me*. When our Dad was dying she sent me away with Alice and James to stay with Granny in Scotland." Even now when she thought of it, she still felt hurt and rejected.

"I dare say your grandmother could have managed James on her own but she'd have found Alice a handful without you to help her."

"It wasn't fair, though."

"Life isn't fair," Albert said in a brisk tone. "Look at this evening. You've had an exciting adventure and Charlie might think *that* wasn't fair, if he knew. Might be best not to tell him, in fact. Not just to be kind to him, but the less talk, the better for everyone. So let's keep it a secret, shall we?"

He was smiling. Humouring her, Jo thought angrily, coaxing her with childish talk about adventures and secrets as if she were Alice!

"Charlie wouldn't be interested anyway. He'd just think it was some sort of game you were playing to make yourself feel important. He doesn't listen to half you tell him, you know. Even if he listens, he doesn't believe it!"

Albert said, "Charlie likes to see things are true for himself. Not just to be told them. He's naturally cautious."

Praising Charlie! Jo said indignantly, "It's not only that."

"No. If you must nail it down, Charlie doesn't want to be told things by *me*. That's understandable. It's hard for a young man his age to be landed with a didactic stepfather. Do you know what didactic means?"

"Like a teacher."

"That's right. I don't get much chance to teach you things, do I?"

"You can teach me how to change subjects," Jo said, and was glad to hear Albert laugh. He hadn't seemed hurt about Charlie, but she was hurt for him.

She said, to Charlie, "Albert knows you don't like him."

They were in bed in their grand hotel room. The little ones were asleep, Alice snoring, James moistly sucking his thumb. Lights from passing traffic patterned the ceiling and Jo saw Charlie's head lift from the pillow.

"You mean you told him I didn't!" He chuckled softly. "It's not really true. I mean, I don't *dislike* him. I'd just like him more if you hadn't gone on and on about how much *you* did. From the beginning."

"I can't see why I should have pretended I didn't, just to please you." She thought of a good thing to say; a good way to make him feel guilty. "One reason I like him, if you must know, is that he makes Mum so happy. Before Albert came, she'd not been. Not for a long time."

Silence. More lights on the ceiling, like delicate lace; horns blowing sadly. Charlie said, "Dad couldn't help making her miserable. He couldn't help dying." He waited for her to answer and when she didn't, because there wasn't an answer to this, he got out of bed and said, "Jo, I've got something to tell you. Come into the bathroom."

"Why? They're fast asleep, James and Alice . . ."

But he was already padding across the room. She pushed

back her covers and followed him. The nylon carpeting was sticky under her feet in the bedroom; the marble floor of the bathroom was cold. Charlie stood by the far door that led to Carrie and Albert's bedroom. He whispered, "They're asleep too. Not a sound." He switched on the light, then sat on the edge of the bath and turned the tap on.

She said, "What are you doing?"

"Turning the taps on. What does it look like?"

"Clever-Dick-Charlie! You know what I meant. I meant *why*."

His face was frowning and serious. He said, "Listen. Something odd happened. You know, when you and Albert went out, we went to the park with the little ones? Well, when we came back, someone had been through our luggage. Not so you'd notice unless you were looking, but one or two things were different. I'd left my case open and someone had closed it. And I'd put my camera on the top, wrapped in my pyjamas. It was still on the top, and wrapped up, but in my red sweater. I told Carrie, and she said, she and Albert had thought that might happen. Expected it, really. It was one of the reasons we'd gone out, she said, to give them a chance to come snooping and get it over! Now they'd had a good look and found nothing, they'd leave us alone for the rest of the holiday. She said she'd tell Albert but I wasn't to worry. *She* didn't seem worried. I asked her what they were looking for and she said she had no idea, nor had they, probably. She seemed to think it was *funny*."

Jo giggled. Charlie said, "What's that for?"

"Nothing. Just you, sitting there running a bath. In the middle of the night."

Charlie closed the taps slowly. Water thumped in the pipes as he whispered, "I thought it was safer. Albert says hotel rooms are bugged sometimes."

"You didn't believe him about that in the taxi. You laughed and pulled faces!"

She wanted to laugh herself, suddenly. But it would make too much noise in the bathroom. She put her hand over her mouth and ran into the bedroom. She got into bed, pulled the clothes over her head and whooped silently into the pillow. Charlie came after her, sat on the bed, tugged at the sheet. She lay on her back and gasped. He said, "What are you sniggering at?"

"You. That's all. Just *you*!" Keeping her laughter in had given her hiccups. She hiccuped and mocked him. "*Albert says, Albert says*! You sneered at me, but you've got the habit now, haven't you?"

Chapter 3

Albert said, "This part of Ithaca is famous for olives. It's the main crop for farmers, though they grow vines, too, and keep sheep and goats. It's quite fertile here—if you look down, to your left, you'll see a stone circle that is used to grind corn—but where we are going, the far side of these mountains, the land is much poorer . . ."

Alice screamed, "Albert, *stop*," meaning the car, not the geography lesson. She jumped up and down. "Look, Albert, the *tortoise*."

It was crossing the road just ahead of them. Albert groaned, "Not *again*," but he stopped the car and they all tumbled out, stretching cramped arms and legs. They had been driving for hours since they left Zenith and were high in the mountains now, so high that although the sun beat down hotly, the air stung cold in their lungs.

Alice ran to the tortoise. It drew in its old, baggy head as she picked it up and crooned to it tenderly. "Poor tortoise, *good* tortoise, don't be frightened of me, I've come to save you."

"That must be about the hundredth time you've made us stop for a silly old tortoise," Charlie complained.

"Only the eighth time," Albert said. "Though I agree, it seems like more, Charlie. And I don't suppose it will be the last. There are an awful lot of tortoises in Ithaca. All busy crossing roads."

"You can't run them over," Alice said, looking indignant. She couldn't bear anything to be hurt, not even a fly or an ant. Once, when Charlie killed a wasp that had stung her she had cried all afternoon. "Poor little wasp, he didn't mean to do anything wrong, it's only his nature." She had buried the wasp in a match-box and put a saucer of jam next to the grave for the wasp's starving children. Now she patted the tortoise's shell as she set it down at the side of the road next to a white shrine with a bottle of oil and a pot of dead flowers in it. "Stupid tortoise, you must learn to keep off the roads or you'll never grow up to be a grandfather."

Charlie laughed at her. "Tortoises don't have families, silly! They lay eggs in holes and go away."

"Everyone has families," Alice said firmly. She squatted down, watching the tortoise as it inched its head out of its shell and began scratching its way, on short, wrinkled legs, through the flowers up the side of the mountain.

There were flowers everywhere, white and purple and yellow, and the cold air smelled sweet.

"It smells of honey and herbs," Carrie said. From the edge of the road, she looked down at the valley. It was empty and peaceful; no traffic in sight, no noise except the humming of insects. Carrie said, "Look. Isn't that a marvellous view?"

James didn't think so. He stood by his mother and sighed. "No shops *anywhere*. And I want an ice-cream."

"You'd only be sick if you had one," Jo said.

"Don't remind him," Carrie said. "We've still got a long way to go."

James scowled. "I'm bored of the car. I expect I will be sick soon."

"Oh James, *no* . . ." Carrie cried anxiously, and James drooped his head.

Albert said, "You can't be sick in a hired car, James. It's not allowed. You'll have to wait until we get to the sea. Then you can go and be sick while we're enjoying ourselves, swimming and exploring and eating our dinner."

James gave him a reproachful look and stumped off, shoulders hunched, kicking up dust. Alice's eyes quivered with tears. "That was mean, Albert. He can't help being sick."

"He'll be sick now," Jo said. "Just to spite us."

"Oh no he won't," Albert said cheerfully. "He's never sick when he thinks he might miss something. Haven't you noticed?"

Carrie laughed and the mountains laughed back at her. The happy echo rolled round the valley. She said, "Albert, what a comfort you are! I do love you!"

Albert blinked, as if shy. He took her hand and Alice skipped beside them as they walked back to the car. Jo and Charlie followed more slowly. Charlie said, "I always knew James put it on. I could have told her."

This wasn't true. They had all believed in James's delicate

stomach. It had started after their father died and had gone on until Albert came. Jo said, "He wasn't sick in the plane. Perhaps he just needed someone to tell him he mustn't be. I mean, someone new. We were all too scared of upsetting him."

"He's upset now, isn't he?" Charlie said. "If he's sick, that'll teach Doctor Albert a lesson."

But James wasn't sick. He was cross when they first got back in the car, staring vengefully at the back of Albert's head with eyes like black stones, but Albert seemed unaware of the menace behind him and talked steadily as he drove, about the place they were going to, an old fortress city called Polis. A history lecture this time and Jo tried to be interested, even though history bored her. It was always the same, nothing but people fighting and killing each other and it seemed strange to her that Albert, who was so kind and gentle, should find it so fascinating. Polis was a famous place once, Albert said, a proud, independent and beautiful city, set on a great rock, with a long, bloody past of heroic battles and sieges. Now all that was left was an ancient tumble of ruins on the top of the rock, a medieval town lower down where people still lived, and a small modern village across the causeway on the mainland where there were shops—"some of them selling ice-cream," Albert said—and one little hotel where they were going to stay.

Alice said brightly, "Will there be monsters, Albert, up on the rock, in the ruins?" She didn't believe in monsters now she was seven but James did, and he perked up and listened.

"I've never seen any myself," Albert said, "but anything's possible. There are certainly plenty of places in Polis where monsters might hide."

James didn't say anything but he cuddled up close to Jo and shivered with pleasure. Then, as they drove through a village, there was so much to see—children running and playing, a herd of goats by a stream, old women perched high on small, dainty donkeys—that he forgot he was meant to be angry and people looked at the car with startled expressions as they saw him grinning and waving. "Not many black faces in Ithaca," Albert said. "You and Alice will surprise the inhabitants, James, you may even frighten them."

Carrie said, "Albert!" in a shocked voice, as if she thought this was something he shouldn't have mentioned but James laughed and rolled his eyes until the whites showed and said, "I'm a Monster Black, I'll scare them and scare them," and growled like a tiger.

Jo said, "You shouldn't encourage him, Albert. He thinks he's special enough already because he's adopted. If you start boosting him up because he's black, too, he'll get too big for his boots any minute."

"Don't be silly, Jo," Carrie said.

Jo was hurt by her tone. She protested, "I was just being *funny*."

Charlie laughed suddenly. "It's no good, Jo. You can't change your skin and there's no point in putting yourself up for adoption elsewhere, so you'll just have to put up with taking second place in this family."

He laughed again, as if this were a joke. Perhaps he had meant it to be, but once out, it didn't sound funny.

Carrie turned round. "What *do* you mean, Charlie?"

He chewed at his lower lip. Jo saw the colour drain from his face and understood the fix he was in. Charlie had been talking about himself! *He* was in second place now Carrie had Albert! But he couldn't say that—it was too painful and private. He muttered, "Oh. Nothing . . ."

Carrie said, very sharply, "You must have meant something."

Charlie turned paler still. He said slowly, "Well . . . You always make more fuss of the little ones than you do of poor Jo. I just thought she might feel she'd be better off if she'd been adopted."

Carrie said, "*Oh,*" as if something, some insect, had stung her. She looked at Jo angrily. "Joanna, how could you!"

This was so unjust, Jo could hardly believe it. She shouted at the top of her voice, "It was Charlie who said it, not me." She saw his desperate eyes, his white face, and knew she couldn't give him away. Instead she said to her mother, "You just turned it round to be spiteful."

Carrie turned to the front of the car. She sat still, staring out of the window.

Albert began to whistle under his breath. No one else made a sound. When Albert stopped whistling, the silence was terrible. Jo longed to escape—open the door and throw herself out of the car! But the road was winding up and up round the mountain like a curling, white ribbon, and when she looked down she felt dizzy. She looked at her mother's profile and said, feeling so bitter the spit had dried in her mouth, "It's not fair. I always get blamed. It's always my fault."

Carrie leaned forward, hands over her face. She whispered, "Oh dear, oh dear, I'm so sorry . . ." and started to cry.

Albert said, "Darling, *don't*— this is so silly, they're just tired, we all are . . ." He stretched out his hand to her—then put it back on the wheel very quickly as a bus appeared round the next bend and hurtled downhill, straight towards them. For a split second they saw the driver quite clearly. He had a wide, curling, black moustache and he seemed to be grinning. A dangling doll attached to the roof of his cab swung backwards and forwards across his grinning face like a pendulum. Albert twisted the wheel. The car lurched off the narrow metal road, skidded on the soft shoulder, and stopped at the edge of the precipice. The bus passed them. Its horn faded to a sad, musical echo as they looked down the drop to the valley. Nothing but blue air beneath them.

For several minutes they sat silent and rigid, hardly daring to breathe in case they rocked the car over. Then Albert said, "That was partly my fault for not paying attention. I apologise. But you've not made it easy in the back, have you? Stopping for tortoises, feeling sick, being sensitive . . . well it's my turn to be *that*, don't you think? I'm human, too. I can put on a display of temperament if I put my mind to it. I'll be grateful if you will abandon family squabbles until we get to Polis and confine your remarks to pleasanter topics. The beauty of the countryside, if you like. Any unusual wild life you happen to notice. If you want information, I'll gladly supply it. Otherwise, keep your mouths shut. Give your mother a rest and me a chance to drive safely."

The children had never heard him speak like that before. Alice's eyes filled up and glimmered like small, dark pools in a rainstorm. She stroked Charlie's knee to make him feel better and he picked up her hand and held it for comfort. James drew up his legs and screwed up his eyes concentrating on not feeling sick. Jo put an arm around him and he nestled against her. She looked at Carrie and Albert and saw them smile at each other. That made her furious. She squeezed James and whispered, "It's all right, poor baby, *I* love you."

This was how they travelled for the rest of the journey; angry and silent. The sun went down and the land grew dark. "Only another few miles," Albert promised, as they left the mountains and bumped in and out of ruts on a straighter, dirt road, but none of them answered. Alice and James were asleep and Charlie and Jo sat with grimly closed mouths feeling lumpish and sullen. And when they stopped finally, there was nothing to cheer them. Albert had said, *a fortress, a beautiful city*, but all they could see when they got out of the car was a great, grim rock sticking up out of a sea that seemed almost solid, more like black jelly than water. A few lights twinkled on the mainland and across the causeway but the rock was dark; a huge, lifeless, menacing mass against the paler night sky.

The hotel was long and low and dimly lit. There seemed to be no one about. A cold, salty wind blew off the water, making them shiver. They stood by the car and looked up at the rock and it seemed to move closer and threaten them. A giant anvil, a vast elephant head with no trunk, floating on the jellified sea . . .

Charlie said, "Where's the fortress?"

"On the other side of the rock," Albert said. "You can see some of the ruins on the top in the daytime but it's too dark now."

"Ruins!" Jo said. "Boring old ruins!" She had expected towers and turrets; fairy castles.

Albert said, rather helplessly, "I'd hoped to get here before sunset. It's so beautiful then. It really is the most beautiful place . . ."

"Seems more like the end of the world to me," Charlie said gloomily. "Cold and dark."

The tone of his voice infected James who started to whimper. "I don't like it here. I want to go home."

"Shut up, you spoiled brat," Jo said, ashamed suddenly. "Poor Albert! He's brought us here for a treat, and we're all being beastly."

"I'm not!" Alice said. "It's just my legs have gone wobbly."

"Tired," Carrie said. "We're all tired, and cold. It'll all

be quite different once we've had a hot bath and some supper".

"No baths, I'm afraid," Albert said. "We'll be lucky if there's hot water. Come on, Charlie, let's get the luggage out."

The hotel had no proper entrance. The door opened into a large, bare room with a few tables, a bar at one end and a television set at the other. As they lugged their bags in, an old woman in black with sunken cheeks and a black patch over one eye came out of the kitchen. Her other eye stared at them balefully; she shouted in a cracked, scolding voice and a young man appeared from behind the bar. Albert dropped the things he was carrying and held out his hands. He said, "Niki!" and the young man embraced him. He had a smooth, smiling, brown face and eyes dark as plums. He and Albert hugged and kissed and laughed loudly, like schoolboys.

Charlie muttered to Jo, "Well, at least we're expected!"

She saw him blush. She said, "Men go in for kissing each other abroad."

"I know. It's just funny. I mean, seeing *Albert* . . ." Grinning, he put his mouth to her ear. "Like this place, it'll take getting used to."

The old woman took them upstairs to a long corridor with only one light at the end and half a dozen rooms off it. She was jolly now, cackling with laughter and prodding Alice and James with brown, knobbly fingers to make them laugh too. They did their best to smile back politely but she was too much like a witch in a picture book, with her one eye and hooked nose and shrunken up mouth to make them feel comfortable. Even Jo was relieved when she gave a last, wild friendly screech and shuffled off down the passage, worn canvas shoes flapping. "Is she the only maid in the hotel?" she asked Albert and was surprised when he said she was Niki's grandmother.

"But she carried the luggage!" Jo said, and Albert explained that in Ithaca the women, even the old ones, did most of the heavy work. "Niki will wait at table and serve at the bar but his grandmother does the cooking and cleaning and carrying. Young men in this country are treated like princes."

"Sounds fine to me," Charlie said, "Jo, you unpack my case and I'll sit and watch you."

She stuck out her tongue. "You'll be lucky. Alice and I are going to share and we'll choose our room! It's Ladies First in this family."

The rooms were all the same: clean and bare with narrow, iron, cot beds and dim, naked light bulbs. There was no bath or shower and the taps of the washbasins clanked when they turned them on and belched out cold, rusty water. "You'll have to keep clean in the sea while we're here," Albert said. "Just wash your hands now, and we'll see about supper."

When they went down there was another guest already eating; a handsome, tanned man with a glistening, bald head and a thick, curling dark beard, tucking into an enormous lobster. Jo looked at him, wondering how it was possible to be so shinily bald and yet grow such hair on your chin. She saw Albert was watching him too, frowning and tugging the lobe of his ear. Then, when the man called to Niki, Albert shrugged his shoulders and sat down at the table.

Jo said, "Did you think it was someone you knew?"

No one else heard her. Carrie was busy settling the little ones and Charlie had disappeared to the lavatory. Albert said, "You don't miss much, do you? Miss Sharp-Eyes! Yes, I did, for a minute. Not so much someone I knew as someone I thought I recognised. Something about him. I was wrong, though. He was speaking to Niki in German."

Niki, passing their table, heard his name and caught Albert's eye. A sharp look before he took the bread and the carafe of wine he was carrying across to the bald, bearded man's table. Albert said loudly, "The lobsters are good here."

The bald man turned in his seat. Niki put the bread and wine down, spread his hands and looked at him, then at Albert. "Herr Schmidt," he said. "Herr Schmidt from Hamburg. Mr Sandwich from London."

Herr Schmidt bowed his head stiffly. Albert nodded and smiled. He beamed round his table. "I think we'll have lobster too, shall we?"

They ate lobster and a tomato and cucumber salad covered in herbs and moistened with lemon juice, and drank a sweetish red wine. Even James had a glass, diluted with water. He sipped at it, dribbling a little with sleepiness, watching the television set crackling away in the corner. A plump jowly man with small eyes was talking and scowling into the camera. "What's he saying, James?" Jo asked, to tease him, and, almost as if he had heard her, the bald German left his seat and turned up the volume.

A rasping, passionate, foreign voice filled the room. James spilled the dregs of his wine and water and the rest of them stopped eating their lobster. Even Alice stopped, the slither of meat Albert had given her out of a cracked claw halfway to her surprised, open mouth. They all stared at the screen and Niki and his grandmother came out of the kitchen and stood staring too, with expressionless faces. The jowly man began waving his arms about and the picture flickered and jumped as if disturbed by his anger. Herr Schmidt bent and switched the set off. He marched out of the room without speaking to anyone.

Niki came to mop up James's spilled drink. He lifted glasses and plates and put a clean paper cloth on the table. He did this in silence, unsmiling, and no one moved or spoke until he had gone.

Then Charlie said, "Who was that on the telly? Bad-tempered old Fat Face."

Albert said, "Please don't shout abuse, Charlie. That was the Dictator."

"*I* knew," Jo said. "Look. His picture's up there. Up over the bar."

They looked where she pointed. At a large, tinted photograph of the same heavy jaw, the same mean, sharp eyes. A wilting garland of greenery hung limply over the top of the frame.

Charlie said, "Why the flowers?"

"A laurel wreath," Albert said. "A conqueror's crown."

Charlie cleaned his plate with a hunk of bread. He said, "I thought Niki was a friend of yours, Albert."

"I've known him a long time. I first came here ten years ago and he was about your age then."

Charlie swallowed his bread. "Does he like the Dictator? I mean, you don't, do you?"

"Friends don't always think the same way. But if you're asking about that portrait, then there's a straightforward answer. All hotels and restaurants are expected to have it hanging up somewhere. If they don't, they're in trouble."

"What sort of trouble?"

"Well, there's no law. But the police can easily find an excuse to close a place down. Niki can't afford that. He has his grandmother to keep, and his mother and sisters in Zenith."

Alice, who had finished her lobster and was beginning to droop, woke up at this mention of families.

"Doesn't Niki's Daddy do that? Is he dead?"

"No." Albert hesitated. "But he's—he's away at the moment. So he can't look after them."

"Is he ill?" Alice persisted. "Is he in hospital?"

"Not exactly . . ." Albert looked at Carrie. It seemed to Jo he was asking for help. Carrie laughed and pushed back her chair.

"Bedtime," she said. "Long past yours, Alice. And poor James is asleep on the table!"

They were all sleepy. Once Jo stood up her legs felt so tired she thought they would never carry her up the stairs. She helped Alice undress and the little girl's eyes were closed before she tucked the blankets up round her. Jo got into her own bed and stretched her toes down to the cold, iron rail at the bottom. Carrie came to say goodnight and opened the window. A soft, seaweedy scent drifted in.

Jo whispered, "Is Niki's father in prison because he's against the Dictator?"

Carrie turned from the window and nodded. Finger to her lips, glancing at Alice.

"It's all right, I won't tell her," Jo said.

Carrie said, "She couldn't keep it to herself. Too exciting."

"Not just that. She'd worry about it."

Alice had fixed ideas about fathers. They should always stay at home taking care of their children. They should never go away, or get sick, or die.

"I think she gets frightened sometimes," Jo said. And then because she could see from the way Carrie's face stiffened that she had said the wrong thing, added quickly, "Look at the way she went on about that old tortoise and his grandchildren! It really worried her to think he might get killed and never see them! Someone's father being in prison would upset her much more. That's why she couldn't help talking about it."

"I hope you won't either," Carrie said. "You know what you are."

She said this cheerfully, as if she meant to be friendly, but Jo was hurt. When Carrie bent to kiss her she turned her cheek coldly and after her mother had gone, lay listening to her voice talking to Albert on the other side of the wall. Was Carrie complaining about her? *You know what she is! Such a cold, wilful girl!* Would Albert stick up for her? Jo held her breath, listening, but she could only hear their voices rising and falling, not what they said. She cried a little, to comfort herself. Perhaps she would die soon, of some dreadful disease. Carrie would weep at her bedside. *I've been unfair to you darling. Please say you forgive me.* But Jo was too tired to enjoy this sad scene; too tired for tears. She yawned until her jaw cracked and rolled on her stomach.

Voices woke her. Voices outside. She got up and went to the window. The moon was high now, trailing a thin wisp of cloud and shining in a long, quivering, silver streak on the black sea. Albert and Niki were standing below her on a concrete strip between the hotel and the shore. Niki said, in English, "It is stupid, of course. To risk everything. But you can understand it. He came for the boy."

Albert glanced up at the hotel and touched Niki's arm. They strolled off along the concrete promenade, heads together. They turned at the end and Niki's cigarette made a red, glowing arc as he tossed it into the water. No one else about, no lights from the town, just the cold moon on the sea and the great, dark rock rising from it. *A fortress*, Jo thought, and then remembering, Niki's father, *a prison*. Such a strange, lonely place. People could be locked away there and forgotten for ever.

The thought made her shiver. She got back into bed and pulled up the covers. Before she went back to sleep she wondered what Niki had meant—who was "the boy" and who had "come for him"—but not very urgently. Experience had taught her that snippets of talk that sounded exciting or interesting were often dull when they were fitted into the whole conversation. And if she still wanted to know, in the morning, she could always ask Albert.

Chapter 4

Cocks crowing. The jubilant sound entered Jo's dreaming mind and became an alarm clock. *School.* Stretching, she stubbed her toes on a hard, iron rail and knew she was not at home. *Where*? She opened her eyes and the room took shape round her; white walls, open window, Alice in the next bed, marble steps in the corner up to a green, shuttered door. The marble was cold under her feet. She pushed the shutters and they opened with a rusty creak on to a balcony. There was the rock and a liquid sun rising behind it, making an orange path on the water.

Albert said, "An improvement on last night?"

He sounded happy. His head was between her and the sun as he peered round the division between the two balconies. Dumb with sleep, she blinked and nodded.

"I'm going up the rock while it's cool. Want to come? Carrie's sleeping."

His dear, rubbery, clown's face was alight with excitement. *He can't wait,* Jo thought, amused. Nothing to do with the weather.

She dressed quickly. Jeans, canvas shoes—last year's, and too small. Albert was waiting in the car outside the sleeping hotel. They drove through the village, past a small harbour. The rock, Jo saw now, was really an island, a craggy, floating mountain joined to the mainland by a rough causeway. "The village is called Polis, too," Albert said. "But old Polis, the medieval town and the ruins above it, are on the other side of the rock, facing out to sea. You can't see them from here. They bumped over the narrow causeway, the road surface pitted and broken, and up round the rock. Barren slopes rose on their left; on their right, the sun struck bright sparks from the sea. Jo couldn't look; her eyes dazzled.

The road came to an end outside the high wall of the fortress. Beyond it, the old town of Polis tumbled down the side of the rock as if an earthquake had struck it. They got out of the car and walked through an archway with stone animals carved on the lintel, into a narrow, climbing, paved street. Old houses with boarded-up windows leaned inwards. A skinny black cat streaked under their feet and bolted over a crumbling wall.

It was a maze, a warren; houses built into the rock like rabbit holes.

"Does anyone live here?" Though there was no one about, Jo felt she should whisper.

"Old ladies and cats," Albert said. "A few rich foreigners, but only in summer."

The tunnels that joined the streets were dank and cold. Something brushed Jo's face; something silky and sticky.

"Spiders," she said. "Lots of spiders here, too."

She thought—*an enchanted, sleeping castle.* Apart from more cats, and the spiders, there was no sign of life except here and there a freshly painted door, a bird in a wicker cage outside a window and once, something horrid, with long, squishy tentacles, dangling from a plastic coat hanger.

"Squid drying," Albert said.

He led the way, up precipitous streets, through cool tunnels, to a large, quiet square where an ancient cannon pointed seaward. Flowering weeds struggled through cracks in the paving and there was an odd smell. Jo sniffed and said, "Liquorice."

"Daisies," Albert said. "Or thistles. I'm never sure which it is."

"Mister Albert-Doesn't-Know-All."

"Boring for me, if I did. Just think, Jo—if you knew everything! Time to die, then."

She laughed, and the sound, in this silent place, startled her. "Why are there so few people? Why did they go?"

"Nothing to keep them. They went to Zenith, or to America. Only the old stayed behind."

Jo said, "Look . . ."

On the far side of the square, stone steps led down through an archway. A bald head appeared; Herr Schmidt, climbing up. At the top he stopped briefly, then turned and ducked back, out of sight.

Jo said, "He's up early."

"So are we."

"He saw us. He didn't want *us* to see *him*!"

"Or just didn't feel sociable. Maybe he likes his own company."

It seemed rude all the same. They had met last night, after all. And it was odd that Albert, who was always polite, should be so quick to find an excuse for his rudeness. He went on, "Some people are naturally solitary. I like Polis best when it's empty, myself. Later on in the day bus loads come, swarming everywhere. Tourists and schoolchildren. This is the best time, I think. Do you feel strong enough to go further up? To the Citadel? Not the very top—just to the church. To Santa Sophia."

He didn't wait for her to answer. He strode eagerly out of the square and she needed all her breath just to follow. As they climbed up steep, broken steps, the medieval town began to spread out beneath them, roofs and domes and little squares, safely tucked inside the enclosing wall of the fortress.

Jo's legs ached, her heart banged—it seemed a terrible effort just to see an old church—but she forced herself on, after Albert. He had asked *her* to come, not Carrie, nor Charlie. Only because she had been awake, of course, but Charlie wouldn't know that and she wouldn't tell him! He'd pretend not to care but he was interested in ruins and history and would feel he'd missed something.

Albert called out, "All right, Jo?"

They were out of the Lower Town now, on a zig-zag path climbing up through real ruins; great, lonely fragments of walls sticking up through tall thistles and waving, blond grasses like giant tombstones in an old graveyard. A vast city once—Jo looked up and saw it, stretching above her to the top of the rock; jagged chunks of pink and grey masonry, deserted and desolate.

Albert said, "Nearly there!" He was waiting for her at a turn in the path beside a twisted, grey tree, flattened on top by the wind. He was holding his hand out. Jo struggled up gasping, feeling she would die if she took one more step. Then Albert said, "There's my girl. Miss Never-Give-Up," and she knew she could go on for ever, climb Everest, as long as he asked her! She would be happy to *die*! As she reached him, she thought—*If I was older, if he was younger, if Dad was still alive to look after Carrie . . .*

She said, "Oh, Albert!" and sighed. He looked down at her gravely and she was scared he knew what she was thinking. She said, in a loud, artificial voice, "Isn't it lovely up here? Look at those butterflies!"

They were everywhere; thousands of tiny, blue wings, the colour of faded jeans, hovering round the grey tree and over the purple-topped thistles. "So small," Jo said, "I've never seen any so small," and waited for Albert to tell her about them.

But all he said was, "They're always up here, round the Church," and continued to look at her with a thoughtful expression as if he was more interested in what was going on in her mind at this moment than in little blue butterflies.

She said nervously, "I've never seen anything like them at all. They must be a most unusual variety." And, when he didn't rise to this bait, "*Albert!* I thought you were going to show me the Church." She widened her eyes and tried to look innocent.

"Oh," he said. "Yes." He grinned and tugged at the lobe of his ear. "I didn't really think you were interested."

As soon as they had turned the bend, past the flat tree, the Church was in view; a flat, tawny dome against the blue sky. A small church, built into the rock. On one side, a sheer drop to the sea.

Albert said, "There's a story. Once, during a siege, the Lower Town was taken and the people fled up here to the Citadel. Some of them hid on top of the rock in the ruins, in the old water cisterns, but those who were too weak or too old to get up there, threw themselves from this place. Old men and old women and children. Mothers jumped with their babies rather than yield to the enemy."

Jo looked down and saw the sea crawling in far below, navy blue in the deeps, and peacock green edged with white lace as it lashed the black rocks. She said, "Oh, I *couldn't.*"

"You'd have been taken into slavery. Or put to the sword."

Jo swallowed and shuddered. "Even then!"

"I agree," Albert said. "I couldn't jump, either. Not even if the Devil were after me. They were a tough lot, the people of Polis. Still are, those that are left of them. If I wanted to raise an army, they're the sort I'd want with me. During the war . . ."

Jo said, "Oh *no*. Not the *war*!"

Albert laughed. "All right. I won't bore you. Just one look in the Church and we'll go back for breakfast."

The Church was neglected and dirty; broken stone columns in corners and a plastic cloth on the altar weighed down at the corners with pebbles. They looked at peeling frescoes on the old walls and a faded painting of a mild, sweet-faced Christ on the underside of the dome. There was a round, metal stand with a few candles flickering. Albert took a thin, yellow stick from a box and lit it from one of the others.

Jo said, "What for?"

He dropped a coin in a tin. "For God. For my family. For all those who died here." He looked at her shyly. "Do you think it's a romantic and meaningless gesture?"

"I don't know." Something more important was bothering her. For a moment, she couldn't place it. When she did, she was frightened. She said, "Those candles. There's no one else here. I mean, we've seen no one . . ."

At the back of the Church, to the side of the altar, a tattered red curtain hung. She pointed and whispered, dry-mouthed, "Albert, it's moving!"

"Just the wind." He pulled it aside. There was no one behind it, just a chair in an alcove and a black robe hanging from a nail in the wall. Albert said, "A priest's hole. I expect a priest comes to say Mass occasionally."

"Do you think he came here this morning?"

"Shouldn't think so." Albert smiled and pushed his glasses

up on his nose. "Perhaps that was what Herr Schmidt was doing. Up here, lighting candles!"

He didn't, sitting on the terrace of the hotel eating breakfast, look much like the sort of man who climbed rocks to light candles in old, ruined churches. Not romantic enough —though perhaps that was just his bald head. Quite apart from his beard, that smooth, naked skull didn't fit with the rest of his face, Jo decided, and when he had finished eating and gone inside, she said so to Charlie. "If Herr Schmidt wore a wig, he'd be really good looking. Like an actor. I mean, he's not really old!"

Charlie pulled a sour face. As she had thought he would be, he was hurt because they had gone off without him. He had sat silent and glowering, barely touching his bread and sweet, runny honey, while the little ones chattered and his parents smiled at each other and made plans for the day. Charlie said, "You could have woken me up!"

He spoke in a grumpy half-whisper, but Albert heard him. He didn't answer directly but started to talk about the Citadel and the blockhouse on the top of the rock which some people thought was Byzantine but which he, Albert, believed was Venetian in origin. He said, "We weren't up to it this morning, but of course the most interesting stuff, archaeologically speaking, is in the Upper Town. I thought Charlie and I might go exploring a bit later on. Too far for Alice and James, and I don't suppose Jo would be keen, exactly. Too much boring history! And a stiff climb."

"I wouldn't mind," Charlie said. He took the last piece of fresh, crusty bread, spread it thickly with butter and honey and nodded at Albert. "Though I think I'd like to swim first."

They swam from a small cove near the hotel, off flat rocks, holed like sponges. The water was cold and clear; looking down they saw their legs waving like pale sea plants above coloured pebbles. Albert blew up Alice's inflatable duck and when she was bored with it Jo lay on its back, floating high in the water, happy and dreaming, until Carrie swam up beside her and said she must put a shirt on to stop herself burning. "Why?" Jo said, scowling, "Why always *me*?"

"Red hair and fair skin," Carrie said. "Not my fault is it?"

Jo flopped off the duck's back and hung underneath, curling her feet round its tail. "Oh, all right," she said, but Carrie was swimming away and didn't hear her.

Jo splashed with her feet, watching the spray fly, and replayed this scene in her mind. Carrie said, "*Jo, honey, your lovely delicate skin. Such a nuisance for you, but you must be careful.*" And she answered, "*Of course, darling Mummy.*"

Jo steered the duck back to the shore very slowly, keeping her shoulders under the water. When she reached the rocks, Albert was waiting. He said, "The others have gone to change. You've stayed in too long, you're all goosey," and put a towel round her, as they walked back, in the broiling sun, to the hotel.

Carrie was on the terrace, talking to two smiling women in floppy sun hats and striped, cotton dresses. One was short and fat, the other tall and thin; they both had kind, bright, beady eyes set in a network of wrinkles and large, happy mouths full of white, even teeth. The tall thin one carried several cameras slung from her shoulders and round her long neck that poked slightly forward, like a giraffe's. She said, in a light, drawly voice, "Is this your daughter? What a beautiful child."

Jo was too embarrassed to speak. Carrie said, "This is Miss Emmeline and Miss Ottoline Skinner. From Arizona."

"Emmy and Tilly," the short fat one said. Her voice was much firmer and deeper than her companion's. "Cousins, not sisters. And delighted to meet you. It is a pleasure to hear English spoken. Tilly and I have no gift for languages and that is a great disadvantage when you want to understand what is going on in a country." She seized Albert's hand and pumped it up and down vigorously as if she were starting an engine.

The tall woman smiled shyly. "Your wife says that you know Ithaca well, Mr Sandwich?"

"As a visitor," Albert said. "Is this your first trip?"

"Yes, indeed," plump Emmy said, beaming. "It is one we had planned for a long time. Long before this dreadful Dictator seized power." Her round face grew solemn. "Naturally, when *that* happened, we debated whether we were right to come! It seemed wrong to appear to approve of a Government that is against Freedom! But then we thought, perhaps we should see for ourselves." She thrust out her chin. "One can always bear witness!"

"Of course," Albert said. He looked puzzled.

Miss Ottoline said in her soft, pretty voice, "My cousin is a journalist. Perhaps the paper is not one you will have heard of, in Europe, but it has quite a ninfluence at home, in our small community."

"It may be small but it's lively," Miss Emmeline said. "And even a little stone can spread ripples if you throw it into a pond hard enough! I hope to gather material for a number of articles and I shan't mince my words. And dear Tilly will take her fine pictures. We understand Polis is really quite beautiful as well as being an ancient stronghold of freedom. We are on our way to the fortress now. We thought we might use it as a background for an interesting piece about the importance of defending democracy. Using photographs of the stout old walls as a symbol."

"It will be very hot in the middle of the day," Albert said.

Miss Emmeline gave a short laugh, like a bark. "Arizona has a fairly fierce climate! We're tough old birds!"

"Not like this child here, with her delicate skin," Miss Ottoline said. She stretched out her thin hand and touched Jo's hair lightly, as if she were blessing her. "It must make you anxious, Mrs Sandwich, seeing her out in this sun."

Carrie's mouth twitched. "Oh yes. Yes, it does."

"You must keep covered up, child," Miss Ottoline said. "And not worry your mother."

She spoke so gently and sweetly that Jo found herself smiling. "Yes," she said. "Yes, I will try." She caught Carrie's eye and they smiled at each other.

Carrie said, "You'd better go and dress now. Wash the salt off."

"And we must be off, up to the fortress," Miss Emmeline said. "It's been good to talk with like-minded spirits. Perhaps we can meet later on, Mr Sandwich, and I can pick your brains about the things that are going on behind the scenes here. Half an hour of your time, if that's not too much trouble? After dinner, perhaps, in the hotel?"

"Certainly," Albert said. "I'll be glad to."

"I must warn you," Miss Ottoline said, "My cousin is a sharp questioner."

The two ladies flashed their good teeth and departed. They climbed into a Volkswagen parked by the terrace and set off with a roar, in a dust cloud. Carrie said, "What a dear, funny pair!"

Albert was frowning. "I hope Miss Emmeline Skinner doesn't ask too many sharp questions of the wrong people. She could get herself into trouble . . ."

"In *Polis*?" Carrie said. "Really, Albert, you are an old Worry-Guts. How could anyone get into trouble in Polis? In this peaceful place!"

It wasn't so peaceful that evening. The Old Town on the rock that had been so eerily quiet when Jo and Albert had walked there that morning was bustling with people now—

standing on doorsteps and talking, or leaning from windows and shouting, or driving small, laden donkeys up and down the steep streets. In the main square a café was open, facing the cannon, and a young, dark-eyed girl served drinks and plates of green olives and white cheese and snippets of salty, smoked fish. Miss Emmeline and Miss Ottoline Skinner were there, reading guide books aloud to each other; men in flat caps smoked and drank small cups of coffee; a party of young priests in black cassocks ate ice-creams and giggled together. Jo said, "Where have they all come from?"

"Off the bus," Albert said. "From the village on the mainland. It's always like this in the evenings."

The sun had gone from the town but struck the rock higher up where a pair of hawks wheeled, stiff winged against the red cliff like tiny, black planes. Talk and laughter rose in the still air that smelled, not of sea, but of flowers. Children in aprons played round the cannon; lean cats stalked the tables, watching for morsels. Alice threw a striped tabby a piece of smoked fish and it growled at the other cats and fled away to feast privately. Emmy and Tilly finished their drinks and left, stopping on their way to tell Albert and Carrie that they intended to climb up to the fortress to take photographs of the higher walls in the sunset.

It was like a picnic, a party. Everyone happy and friendly together. Then a puzzling thing happened. As if at some pre-arranged signal, a strange silence fell. It was like Zenith, Jo thought, when the Dictator drove by. One minute, a cheerful, talkative town; the next, a cold, watchful silence . . .

But this wasn't Zenith. There was no motorcade, no black limousine, no sirens, no soldiers. Only one young, rather fat policeman in a tight-fitting, grey uniform, walking into the square. He wore a gun round his waist in a brown, leather holster and carried in his right hand a tall, stiff, single lily.

He nodded and smiled at the company as he crossed the square to the café but no one responded. He sat at a table, ignored and alone, awkwardly holding his white, waxen flower, and after a little people began talking again, but more quietly, leaning towards each other as if what they had to say was suddenly private. The policeman rapped on the table and the dark-eyed girl came for his order. She stood beside him, a pretty girl in a faded, blue cotton dress, and he smiled at her and held out the lily. For a second she hesitated, looking at the flower, at his eager, hot face, then glanced over her shoulder. A sharp voice shouted, "Elena!" The girl ducked her head and ran back into the café and an old woman came out to serve the policeman instead. He sighed and put the lily down on the table.

Alice whispered, "He brought that flower for that girl. It was mean not to take it."

Carrie said, "It's none of your business. Why don't you and James go and play with the children, over there, round the cannon."

Alice looked scornful. "They don't speak English. They're stupid."

"Perhaps they think you are. Not speaking their language."

James slipped off his chair and walked cautiously towards the cannon. The children were straddling the barrel and pushing themselves along with their hands. They looked at James sideways and giggled but allowed him to join them. One of the bigger ones even helped him up on the cannon and showed him where to place his hands. He sat, thin legs dangling, face screwed up and serious.

Carrie said, "Look at James, Alice." But Alice was watching the policeman. He was sipping a glass of pale lemonade, his plump face pink with embarrassment. Alice said, sadly, "No one wants to be friends with him."

Charlie said, "People don't like the police much in Ithaca. Ask Albert. He'll tell you."

Albert said, "This part of the country is very strongly against the Dictator. They trust no one in uniform."

"The girl would have taken his flower," Alice said. "Only that horrible witch-person stopped her. It's not fair! The poor policeman!"

She sat straight-backed in her chair, looking indignant and beautiful and Carrie and Albert smiled at each other, over her head, then at Herr Schmidt who had suddenly appeared beside them. He bowed, clicking his heels, and said, in careful English, "A lovely evening is it not? I hope you are enjoying your holiday in this most strange and wonderful place. I myself am here for historical reasons—I am interested in ancient times—but I expect you have come for the sea and the swimming."

Albert laughed—for no reason that Jo could see—and said,

"Yes, Herr Schmidt, we are here on a family holiday." He gestured at James's empty chair. "Won't you join us?"

Herr Schmidt shook his bald, bullet head. "You are kind, but I would not wish to intrude on your privacy. Time spent alone with one's family is precious. I know." He bowed to Carrie again, walked to the policeman's table, bowed to him, and sat down. He ordered a drink from the witch-like old woman, took a map from his pocket and spread it out on his knees.

Charlie said, "Have we got a map? We could do with one in this town. It's like a maze."

"I did have one," Albert said. "I lost it in Zenith."

Charlie looked at him. "You mean it was pinched from the luggage?"

Albert frowned a warning, nodding at Alice. But she wasn't listening. She had got down from her chair, eyes still fixed on the policeman. He was eating an ice now, leaning forward, fat knees spread, to avoid dropping it on his uniform. Alice advanced slowly towards him, step by furtive step, as if she were playing Grandmother's Footsteps.

Charlie said, "Whatever *for*, Albert?"

"No idea, Charlie. Unless they thought it might have secret marks on it."

"Arms dumps, that sort of thing?"

"Well." Albert smiled. "Perhaps. It could have been just that whoever it was did the job, searched the room, thought he had to take something back. I've long ago given up trying to fathom what the Dictator's minions think they are up to."

"Is *he* one of them?"

Albert followed his gaze. "The policeman? Yes, I suppose so. He'll be small fry, of course, but they must think he's reliable or he wouldn't be stationed here. Polis may be a small place but it has a reputation for independence. This is wild country, a long way from Zenith. That man will keep his eyes and ears open and report the first sign of trouble."

"What trouble?"

"Counter revolution is what the Dictator's afraid of."

Carrie said, "Those that live by the sword know they will die by the sword!" Her eyes flashed like green lights; her voice was high and excited.

Albert smiled at her. "That sort of thing, yes. But the policeman will report anything. Any unusual activity. Idle talk at the café . . ."

Charlie said, "Do you think he speaks English?"

"Almost certainly. I daresay he knows who we are—he'll have looked at our passports. You remember we had to hand them in, at the hotel? But he won't bother us as long as we don't talk too loud and don't go round inciting the locals. It's them he's watching. That's why no one will have anything to do with him."

"I know that," Charlie said. "I'm not stupid."

"No. Sorry, Charlie."

Albert grinned at Charlie and, after a second, Charlie

grinned back. Jo felt left out. She wondered if Albert thought *she* was stupid. She said, "He must be a horrible man to spy on people like that. *I* won't have anything to do with him either!"

Carrie laughed. "Someone will, though! Look at Alice!"

She was standing by the policeman's chair, staring up at him with round, sympathetic, dark eyes as he finished his ice and wiped his hands on a red handkerchief. She waited there, quiet as a mouse—or as one of the crouching cats under the table. In the end, he looked down at her, and she said, "Hallo, I'm Alice. *I* like your beautiful flower."

He looked startled and shy. He finished wiping his hands and tucked his handkerchief away in his pocket. He picked up the lily, and hesitated. Alice smiled at him boldly and sweetly. He returned her smile, with a slow blush of pleasure, and gave her the lily.

Chapter 5

The great rock was black when they woke in the mornings, the saffron sun rising behind it; a washed-out, silvery grey in the daytimes and red in the evenings. When the light left the sky it stole back to the land and turned the cliffs rosy. They had been lucky, so Albert said. At this time of year, in the springtime, there were often high winds and rough seas. Sometimes the top of the rock was hidden in storm clouds for days. He said, "Make the best of it. It may turn cold any minute."

The children groaned. Grown-ups were always on about weather. They trusted it; saw no reason why it should change. The golden days passed, merging into each other, so that after a week it seemed they had been there for ever. As if they had always woken to still, beautiful dawns with a hushed, gentle sea creeping silkily in and breaking in whispering waves on the shore; always swum for hours after breakfast; always slept in the breathless, afternoon heat; always crossed the causeway to the Old Town in the evenings to explore the cool, tunnelled streets, the tiny, tucked-away churches, the small, silent squares. Finding, every day, something new . . .

Jo met Alexis on the ninth day. She was alone. Charlie had stayed at the hotel because Niki had promised to let him ride his motor scooter on the promenade before dinner. Carrie and Albert had arranged to meet the American ladies, Miss Emmeline and Miss Ottoline Skinner, for a drink at the café in the Old Town square, and the little ones were playing with the local children round the cannon. The different language didn't bother James. It didn't bother Alice, either—when she wanted to organise a new game she simply shouted more loudly than usual in English—but she had really decided to stay in the square to watch for her fat policeman friend. He came to the café most evenings, often bringing her something, sweets or a bunch of wild flowers, and sometimes she sat on his knee.

Jo said, this evening, "He won't always come, Alice," and then, louder, for Albert's benefit, "You shouldn't always hang around waiting, he'll think you're expecting a present," but Alice ran to hang upside down on the cannon and Albert seemed not to have heard her.

Jo wandered off, feeling lonely. They all had friends except her. She was ugly, that was probably why! And she turned pink as a shrimp, not brown, in the sun! She climbed a flight of stone steps, sweat trickling down the back of her knees, and heard voices in her head saying, Look at that *pink, plain, stupid girl. Does she think she is pretty, just because she's got that red hair*!

There was no one about. This part of the town was high up, a long way from the café which was at its centre, and the houses all looked deserted. Some of the boards on the windows had rotted; she pushed a plank to one side and peered into a tiny, dark hovel that was full of old, iron bedsteads. She let the plank fall back into place and walked round the side of this house, along a shaded, narrow path, overgrown with tall thistles. There was a rank, goaty smell, and then, at the end of the path, a smell of herbs and wild grasses. She came into a sunny square that looked over the sea. An old, gnarled, twisted fig tree grew in the centre with a bell hanging from it. Spiders' webs hung from the fat, moist, grey leaves like fine, lacy shawls. She poked a hole in one of the webs and watched the spider scutter to safety.

Behind her, someone said, "Don't touch that bell!"

She flung round, heart thumping. She had done nothing wrong but she felt she had been caught out in something. She half expected to see Alice's friend, the fat policeman, but it was only a boy; a tall, thin, handsome boy with thick, shining, dark hair, wearing a white shirt, jeans, and white sandals. He said, "It is the old school bell. There used to be a school here once, long ago. Now the bell must only be used for emergencies. To summon the people in time of danger."

"Like a fire?"

"Or an attack from outside. To warn them to close the gates against an invasion." He smiled and she thought—*He's not handsome, he's beautiful*! She had never in her life seen such a beautiful boy. His face, polished brown by the sun, was fine and sharp as a face etched on an old coin, or a medal. He said, "I have never heard it rung in my lifetime."

"Do you live here?"

"My family have a holiday house. We come for a short time in the spring, then for the whole of the summer."

He had an accent she couldn't place. Albert had said some rich foreigners owned houses in Polis. She said, "I meant, where is your *home*?"

"Zenith, of course." He looked surprised as if it had never occurred to him that he might live anywhere else. "We have a flat in what used to be Democracy Square. It is now called the Place of the New Revolution but we will change the name back again when we have overthrown the Dictator."

He spoke calmly and clearly. There was no one to hear but she thought he would not have cared anyway. He would have spoken like that, like a proud young prince who was frightened of no one, if the square had been crowded with soldiers. She said, "You should be more careful how you talk to strangers. You don't know who I am. I might tell someone what you've just said. I might be a spy."

He laughed. "I don't think you are. You are an English girl, aren't you? I have seen you several times with your family. Your brother, and the two African children."

"They're not African. Alice was born in London and James is a Scot from Edinburgh. My parents adopted them. Have you been watching us?"

He didn't reply for a minute. He dug his toe into a crack in the paving, kicked out a small stone and dribbled it, with some fancy footwork, towards the parapet on the seaward side of the square. He sat on the parapet and turned back to her. "I have been following you all this last week. Round and round the town and up to the Citadel. I am very clever. You didn't see me!"

She thought of him, tracking her through the narrow streets, watching and listening. She wasn't sure if she was flattered or angry.

He said, "I think your mother is beautiful. I noticed her first."

"Oh."

"Then I saw you and your brother and heard you speaking in English. I thought it would be pleasant to talk to you. I speak excellent English but it would be good practice. And I am not allowed to make friends among the young people who live here. That is lonely for me but it would be dangerous for them, so I have to suffer."

He sighed pointedly and gazed out to sea with a tragic expression that irritated her. She thought—*I won't ask him questions, he's boasting*. But she couldn't resist it. She said, "Why should it be dangerous?"

He said, "My name is Alexis Platonides."

He jumped off the parapet and stood facing her, proudly smiling. She shook her head, feeling stupid. "I'm sorry. I mean, I don't know . . ."

"Then I will explain to you. My father is Andreas Platonides. He is famous in Ithaca. He has been living in exile for more than two years now but everyone knows he will come back one day and rouse the people up against the

Dictator. My father is a great Democrat. He was an important man in the Government when the Dictator took over and he would be dead or in prison now, if he had not been abroad on a mission when it all happened."

He looked at her with bright, pale, grey eyes and she saw herself reflected in them. His smile died and he said, in a low voice, "It was horrible. The soldiers went to arrest all the members of the Government in the early hours of the morning. They came to our flat for my father and when my mother said he was out of the country they were very angry. They said the Dictator and the Army were taking over because the Government had betrayed the people. They said the Government were all Communists. I said that was a lie, and one of them hit me and made my nose bleed. I thought they would arrest us then but they only threw things about in the flat and shouted and ordered my mother to make coffee for them. My mother was frightened. When they went, she said we must leave at once. We packed a suitcase and caught the ordinary bus to the airport but when we got there, they stopped us. They locked us in a room for five hours without anything to drink, although it was very hot, and then, in the end, a man came—one of the Secret Police, not a soldier—and said my mother could catch the next plane to New York if she wanted to. Since she was born in America and had an American passport they couldn't prevent her. But I must not leave. My mother cried and begged the man to let us both go but he said I must stay as a hostage, a guarantee of my father's behaviour. My mother said, in that case she would stay too, and we were sent back to the flat in a car. Maria, our maid, was there, crying. She said the soldiers had come for my father's things, all his papers and books, and when she tried to stop them they beat her. Since then, they have left us alone, but they watch us. No letters ever come through the post from my father, only sometimes by hand, when his friends come and arrange to deliver them secretly, and they watch us wherever we go. They watch me, particularly. They believe my father will not dare plot against the Dictator while I am here, under their eye . . ."

He smiled suddenly, brightly and impishly, as if he knew better. Jo caught her breath as she remembered the letters Albert had brought. Albert the Postman! She said, "What would happen to someone who brought you a letter? If they were caught, I mean."

"They would be arrested, of course." He shrugged his shoulders as if this was a silly question.

"Even if they were foreigners?"

"That would not save them. They call my father an Enemy of the State. In Ithaca, it is a crime to bring letters from him to his family and whoever does is a criminal here. If I stole something in England I would be treated as a thief, wouldn't I? Even though I didn't live there."

"Stealing's different."

He laughed. "Not to *them*!"

She burst out, "But they wouldn't send someone who carried letters to *prison*! I mean, that's ridiculous. If that's *all* that they'd done . . ."

She stopped. He was looking at her with a puzzled, searching expression as if wondering why she felt so strongly about something that couldn't concern her and she was suddenly frightened. Albert had known what he was doing in Zenith was dangerous. He had told her to keep it a secret. And she had almost let it out to this boy! Suppose someone had heard her! The sweat broke cold on her forehead; she wriggled her shoulders and gave a loud, foolish laugh that echoed in the quiet square. "I just meant it seemed pretty crazy to me! Like your not being able to make friends with people in Polis! I mean that really *is* crazy. You're only a boy!"

He said coldly, "And you are a silly girl. I thought you had understood me. I will tell you again, so please listen this time. It is all right in Zenith. There I may go to school and have friends just as always. The Dictator knows who he cannot trust and it is easy for his spies to watch them. Here it is different. There is only one policeman and the soldiers have a long way to come. My family is allowed one old servant but anyone who spent a lot of time at our house or was seen talking to me would be reported at once. The Dictator cannot afford to take chances. If the people of Polis rose up against him he would have a war on his hands."

Jo stared at the ground, cheeks and ears burning. He had called her a silly girl! She would never forgive him. She muttered, "You need guns for a war."

"You think we don't have them?"

She gasped and looked up at the rock where the birds

dived and squabbled in the soft, evening light. She thought —*Arms dumps*! Could they really have been marked on Albert's map that was stolen in Zenith? Oh, of course not. Albert had been quite calm when Charlie suggested it. And he would never have brought them all here if he'd thought there was any danger. Then she remembered he had taken her with him, deliberately, when he delivered those letters. If he were a spy, after all, a wife and family would be excellent cover . . .

Alexis said, "The Dictator has a house on an island not far from here. Sometimes he flies over Polis in a small plane. They have a ground-to-air missile hidden up in the Citadel. The next time he comes they will shoot him down. Then my father will make a new Government and we will be free again."

His voice sounded different. Jo looked at him sharply and saw that his grey eyes were dreamy.

She said, "You're making that up!"

"Perhaps." He giggled and it made him seem very much younger. "You cannot know that!"

"I can tell. I knew you were telling the truth about what happened to you and your mother. It sounded true. What you said just now doesn't." She chose words to wound him. "It sounded pure childish nonsense."

He scowled. "I am older than you."

"How old are you?"

"Fourteen." He hesitated. "I shall be fourteen in two months. I think you are not so old yet."

"Girls are always older than boys of the same age. That's an established, biological fact."

"So you are younger than me."

"That's not what I said."

Alexis giggled again. "My father says I am extremely mature for my age."

"I thought he hadn't seen you for more than two years!"

He screwed his eyes up and was quiet for a moment. Then said, "He said I was mature before he went away. When I was eleven."

"Perhaps you've gone backwards since then."

"I have not!"

"You wouldn't know, would you?"

He stamped his foot and shouted, "My father says I am a genius!"

This was so absurd she wanted to laugh. But he was angry and serious. She said, keeping her face straight, "Don't be silly."

"I AM NOT SILLY."

She put her head on one side and considered his furious face. "In that case, there isn't much point in your talking to me, is there? I mean, if you're a *genius* and I am a *silly girl*! We can't really have too much to say to each other."

She started to walk out of the square. It was an effort not to look back but she managed it. She ran along the dank, thistly path and round the small house where the iron bedsteads were rusting.

He caught her up at the top of the flight of stone steps. She marched steadily down, face averted. He leapt ahead and ran backwards in front of her. "Please don't go like this. Please don't be angry."

She said, "Do be careful. You'll break your neck if you fall backwards."

"I won't fall. I am like a mountain goat, light and sure on my feet."

"Pride goes before a fall."

"Don't make me fall, then."

He stopped, barring her way, and smiled his bright, beautiful smile. "Would you like to come to my house? My mother is in Zenith, but our old maid is there so it would be quite proper! We could play records."

"I can't, it's too late. My parents will be waiting for me at the café. It's time to go back for dinner."

"Tomorrow, then? If you go down from the square, down the steps facing the sea, you will come to my house. There is a stone leopard carved over the door and a tall cypress tree in the garden."

"I might."

"*Please.* I have no one to talk with. And I will tell you something, I promise. A secret. It wasn't true about the ground-to-air missile, that was a game I thought up, but something exciting is going to happen quite soon and I know all about it."

"Suppose I don't want to know!"

"Then of course you won't come." He stood aside to let

her pass and as she did so, caught her arm and said in a loud whisper, "If you don't want to know, send your brother. It is the sort of secret boys like to share."

She shook herself free. She tried to be angry but his face danced with such delight at his own clever teasing, she couldn't be cross with him. He was a strange boy, she thought—so grown up one minute, so childish the next. He made her feel quite old and protective. "All right," she said, "I'll come tomorrow."

She went on, down to the main square. He called after her, "If you don't come to my house I will wait the same time, the same place, up by the bell," but when she turned round to wave, he had vanished. She shouted, "I'll be there," but the rock above threw her voice back and there was no other answer.

Carrie and Albert were sitting on the sea wall and watching the sun slip out of sight like a ball of red jelly. Jo panted up and said she was sorry to keep them waiting. Usually she found it hard to apologise but now, for some reason, the words came out easily. "I didn't look at my watch, I was having such a good time." She half-hoped they would ask her what she'd been doing but they just smiled and said it didn't matter, there was no real hurry. "Glad to rest up a bit," Albert said. "I've had an exhausting experience. Giving a history lecture to Miss Emmeline Skinner."

"She lectured *you*," Carrie said. "That's what you found tiring."

They called Alice and James from their game round the cannon and walked slowly out of the Old Town. Outside the high wall, Alice's policeman was talking to one of the ancient women who haunted the town. They all looked much alike in their black dresses and old, floppy slippers, but Jo thought she would recognise this one the next time she saw her. She was laughing at something the policeman had said, withered lips drawn back over purple gums with a few brown, rotten teeth planted jaggedly in them. Jo looked away from this horrid sight but Alice waved cheerfully. The woman cackled with laughter like a very old hen and the fat policeman grinned and said, "Good evening, Miss Alice."

"He likes me," Alice said confidently as they got in the car. "He likes having a friend, that's what he told me. He's got two brothers and two sisters. One of his brothers sells fur coats in Zenith, the other one is a sailor, and his sisters are married. He hasn't seen them for a long time. He hasn't seen his mother or father either, and he misses them very much. He has a dog at home and he misses him, too."

The car wouldn't start. Albert got out and looked under the bonnet. Carrie got out too, and stood watching him. Alice bounced about in the back of the car. She said, "Hurry up, Albert." She knelt on Jo to lean out of the window and waved to her policeman.

Jo said, "You're squashing me."

"I'm just saying goodbye," Alice said. "He likes me to wave to him. He's so sad to be living here, so far from his family. It's like being an orphan."

Her sharp knees dug into Jo. She pushed her off crossly and said, "Stop going *on*, Alice. It's not *very* sad. After all, he's grown up! *I've* got a friend here who hasn't seen his father for ages and ages and that really *is* sad because he's only a boy."

Alice sat back on the seat, legs stuck out in front of her. "What's his name?"

"Alexis. He's fourteen, the same age as Charlie. Perhaps a bit younger."

"Where's his Daddy?"

"Abroad somewhere." It was too hard to explain why to Alice. "He hasn't been home for more than two years."

Alice looked at her with sad, soft, brown eyes. She said, "Oh, poor Alexis," and Jo laughed and hugged her.

Albert got back in the car. He said, "That should do it." He pressed the starter and the car juddered. "Clever old me," Albert said, and leaned across to open the passenger door. Carrie got in, shivering. She said, "There's a wind getting up."

"Weather's changing," Albert said, "I told you it might, didn't I?"

Chapter 6

Although the sun was still bravely shining next morning, a greyish cloud perched on the top of the rock and the sea tore in at the foot, throwing up white fangs of spray. Gulls dived like darts over choppy waves in the bay and a steamer that had docked in the night rocked by the harbour wall. Niki, serving breakfast coffee and bread, told them it was a German cruise ship. "They come for the day," he said, "for a swim and to visit the Citadel."

It seemed rough for a swim but while they were eating, the passengers came off the ship and strolled round the harbour and along the concrete promenade in front of the hotel, to the rocky pool. They were all quite old but they dived off the flat, volcanic rocks, laughing loudly and splashing each other and shouting, "Wünderbar!"

"Like a lot of kids," Charlie said scornfully.

"Cooped up in a ship, poor things," Carrie said. "I expect they're glad to get off it."

Nothing much happened at Polis. No one passed through because the road ended there, the ordinary steamer only called once a week and only in summer, and there was only one daily bus. All new arrivals were therefore regarded with interest and a straggle of townspeople, old men and old women and children, had followed the bathing party from the harbour. They stood on the shore, watching the swimmers hurling themselves enthusiastically in and out of the water, and the hotel guests watched from the terrace. Niki's grandmother emerged from the kitchen and glared with her one eye and Miss Ottoline Skinner went down to the rocks with her cameras. Miss Emmeline followed her, stopping to say good morning to Carrie and Albert. She said she was sorry the weather had changed, for their sakes, though of course Tilly was pleased because cloud effects were artistic. She looked at her cousin, crouching on the rocks to take pictures of jolly, elderly bathers, and said thoughtfully, "One can never be sure what will prove important. I have often thought, if Tilly had been there when our President was assassinated, taking photographs of the crowd, she might easily have got a chance shot of his murderer."

Albert looked seaward. "I hardly think . . ."

"One doesn't, *beforehand,*" Miss Emmeline said darkly. "Those people all look very innocent but that was precisely my point!" Albert and Carrie looked at her, startled, and her kind, beady eyes kindled. She leaned closer and said, sinking her already deep voice to a gruff rumble, "If I wanted to enter this country to despatch the Dictator, one good way to escape notice would be to come disguised as a tourist!"

She winked at Charlie, who laughed. When she had gone after Tilly, he said, "She's a joker!"

"Only half, I think," Jo said. She looked at the American

lady's plump, determined, dignified back and was fascinated. She couldn't be certain but she thought Miss Emmeline Skinner had been partly pretending, partly believing, the way she did herself when she was imagining some exciting adventure. She said, in a surprised voice, "But Miss Skinner's *old* . . ."

Albert said, "The nicest people never grow up altogether." He spoke rather absently, looking beyond her to the end of the terrace where Herr Schmidt sat alone, eating his breakfast, and Niki was laying extra tables with cups and glasses and plates in case the visitors should need refreshment after their swim. When he had finished, he changed his white jacket for a fresh one, checked that he had a pad and a pen in his breast pocket, and said, to Herr Schmidt, "It is possible none of them will speak English. If they come, you will interpret, perhaps? I cannot speak German."

Herr Schmidt stood up abruptly, pushing his chair back. He said, "I have completed my meal. Someone among the boat party will be able to make their wants clear to you."

Behind his back, Niki grinned at Albert and spread his hands ruefully. Herr Schmidt looked at Albert too, and then, as if he sensed he had been somewhat graceless and wished to make up for it, smiled and said, "My countrymen are very hardy. I would not advise you to swim here today. There is an undertow on this coast that would be too strong for your children."

"Do you know this place well?" Albert asked.

"I used to visit it often. Of course the sea does not change, but other things do. I have not been to Ithaca for almost three years and I have found much that is different." Herr Schmidt stood by their table, stroking his beard; his eyes rested on Albert with what might have been, if he had not been such a humourless person, a gleam of amusement. "In many ways, I find that the changes have been for the better. There is more order in the way things are done, much more discipline. The towns and hotels are much cleaner, which is good for the tourist trade, and there are many fine new roads everywhere."

"Most of them are not finished," Albert said.

"Give them time. Rome was not built in a day and this new, strong Government has made a good start. Zenith, you must agree, is a pleasanter place. I can remember when everyone sat about gossiping in the cafés and nothing got done. Now the roads are swept, business attended to. Even the trains run on time."

"And all the tiresome people who might make trouble about free elections and free speech and that sort of thing have been tidied away out of sight."

Albert spoke in a cheerful tone and Herr Schmidt nodded approvingly. "Inefficient countries cannot afford those kind of freedoms."

"No, indeed!" Albert said.

Jo was appalled. Had Albert gone *mad*? How could he agree with this awful, bald man, when poor Niki was standing there listening just a few yards away. Niki's father was one of those people who been "tidied away out of sight". Had Albert *forgotten*? She said, "You don't believe that. You know the Dictator is a wicked man, Albert. You *told* us. Spying on people and sending them to prison just because they say things against him!"

"Did I tell you that?" Albert's face was impassive; she couldn't tell what he was thinking.

"You know you did!" As she thumped her fist on the table, the angry blood thumped in her head. She glared at Herr Schmidt. "He was just being polite to you!"

"I am obliged." Though this was stiffly said, Herr Schmidt did not seem offended. He was still stroking his beard—and watching her with an interested expression. Then he lifted his head and looked at the first of the bathers, walking up from the shore. He came on to the terrace, a large, middle-aged man, healthy and smiling. He smiled at them all and said, "Guten morgan."

Herr Schmidt turned and left the terrace.

Charlie looked after him. As more bathers swarmed up, laughing and chattering, he said, "That's strange, isn't it? You'd have thought he'd have stopped for a minute."

Albert said, "Perhaps he didn't feel like talking."

"He was talking to *us*."

Jo said, "I shan't talk to him, not ever again. I think he's a horrible person."

She felt sick with rage and an odd kind of shame. She had trusted Albert, believed he was perfect. What a fool she had been! Albert knew what Herr Schmidt was saying was wrong but he had just sat there meekly. Oh, that was shameful! She was ashamed of him!

She said, "You're a traitor."

Albert pushed his glasses up on his nose and sighed. That was all—just a sigh.

She said, "You should have *told* him. You said you were a coward, Albert, and I didn't believe you, but I do now."

She felt the tears heaving up in her chest; she couldn't stop them. Bolting from the table, she wept with her mouth open. The wind rushed into her open mouth and blew her hair over her face as she ran. She scraped her ankle getting over the sea wall and drops of blood oozed in a line like beads on a string. She sat on the rocks, pretending to examine her wound, and the sea groaned in the fissures and flew up and drenched her. Salt spray and salt tears mingled and dried on her cheeks.

After an age Charlie came. He sat beside her and said, "Don't cry, Jo."

"I shan't ever listen to a single word Albert says. Never, never, as long as I live."

Charlie said, "Albert did tell Herr Schmidt what he thought, but in a sly sort of way. There's no point in quarrelling with someone like that. Just for the sake of it. You can't change some people."

"He could have tried, couldn't he?"

"Perhaps Albert thought he was entitled to his opinion. I suppose there is something to be said on the other side. Nothing's all bad."

"It's one thing to argue. I mean, in a school debate. When you know someone who's caught up, it's different."

"You mean Niki? His father in prison?"

She shook her head. "I just said that. I was thinking of someone else. A boy I met on the rock."

Telling Charlie the story, it seemed sadder than when she first heard it. It made her start crying again. Words and tears bubbled together. ". . . then they hit him, and he was only a little boy. He was brave, though. Not like Albert. He said the soldiers were liars . . ."

Charlie said, "I think Albert might be quite brave if it mattered." He paused, then went on rather shyly, "You were a bit unkind, really."

She felt so miserable, she thought she would die of it. She would stay here on the rock until the sea came up and drowned her. She could never go back to the hotel; she couldn't even look back, in case Carrie and Albert were watching.

She said, "Were they very angry?"

"No. When you ran off, Carrie said, *good for her*!"

"*Did* she?"

"She laughed," Charlie said. "Then she said, *that'll teach you, Albert-The-Good. People who perch on pedestals are bound to fall off some time or other.*"

"That was mean!"

"I thought so," Charlie said. "It's not Albert's fault you think he's so wonderful."

"I don't any longer."

"That's what I meant."

"Oh . . ." She wasn't sure how she felt. A bit spiteful and sore still, but sad too, as if she had lost something. She said, "Did Albert mind?"

"A bit, I think. He didn't say anything. Just made that grunt in his throat and got out the map to decide where they are going today. They're taking a picnic inland to look at some ruins since the weather's so bad here. I said I'd stay with you because you wouldn't be interested."

"*You* would be though, wouldn't you?"

Charlie shrugged. "If you'd rather I went, there's still time. I mean, if you'd rather keep your friend to yourself, I don't mind."

"No, of course not, why should I?" She opened her eyes wide and let her jaw drop, acting astonishment.

"Aw, come *off* it," Charlie said.

She was afraid she was going to blush. She stood up and stepped to the edge of the rocks, lifting her face to the wind and the spray. She said, "He's about your age, but I expect he'll seem young to you. He's a bit spoiled and boastful. He thinks he's a genius. That's what his father has told him and I'm afraid he believes it."

She wondered what Charlie would think of Alexis. Part of her wanted them to meet, and part of her didn't. She said, "You may simply hate him."

Niki took them up to the Old Town on the back of his bike.

The wind was so cold it was like flying through a cloud of small, stinging insects; Charlie clung to Niki and Jo clung to Charlie, burying her icy face in his sweater. The bike shuddered and lurched over pits in the road; at one bend, they swerved through a small herd of goats and a wild looking girl with bare feet leapt off the rock, screaming shrill as a sea bird, and threw a shower of stones after them.

The town gate was sheltered from the worst of the gale but they could hear the sea far below, sucking and thudding as if it would break the rock loose from its moorings. Niki said, "If the wind drops, there will be mist on the top, so be careful." He waved and roared off, revving dramatically.

When he had gone, they felt lonely. The town was almost as empty as it had been the first morning; no tourists; doors and windows shuttered against the bad weather. The few people abroad in the streets looked at them sullenly as if they had no business there. One old man, wolf-faced under his greasy, flat cap, glared with such venom that even when they had passed, they felt his eyes boring into them.

Charlie gave an uneasy laugh. "He looked as if he was wondering what sort of meal we'd make. Albert says, once during a siege, rather than give in to the enemy, the people here ate their children. Sold them to each other at so much a pound and stewed them up with seaweed for flavour."

"*Yuk!*" Jo felt her stomach shrink. "Let's go home."

"Alexis won't eat us? Or will he?" Charlie rolled his eyes and smacked his lips. "Perhaps that's why he made friends with you. Luring another young girl to the cooking pot!"

"Don't be silly!"

All the same, when they found the house after a search through the maze of streets down the steps from the square, Jo was reluctant to pull the wrought-iron bell. The heavy, brass-studded door was shut and secret like the door to a castle, and the crouching stone leopard carved over the portal had a realistically menacing air—as if it might come to life and tear at their flesh any minute. As Charlie tugged and made the bell jump and jangle, Jo hung back behind him, ready to run, and when the old woman opened the door, her first thought was that she looked thin and hungry . . .

Then she recognised her. She was the old woman who had been talking and laughing with Alice's policeman. Pointed brown teeth jutted sharp from her gums as she grinned in welcome. Jo faltered, "Alexis?" and the old woman flung her head back and screamed his name into the dark house behind her. Then she looked at Jo and Charlie and cackled.

Alexis appeared. He was wearing a purple shirt and matching purple sandals. The old woman let out a torrent of what sounded like wild abuse, and he shouted back at her in her language. He said, to Jo, "She says I have not finished my violin practice, the meddling old idiot." He pushed her aside and came into the street, slamming the door. He eyed Charlie. "Is this your brother?" he asked, and went on, before Jo could answer, "I play the violin very beautifully, even better than I play the piano, but I must practise for at least two hours every day to become really excellent."

"Don't let us stop you. I mean, I would hate to think we had deprived the world of a musical genius."

Charlie spoke in his most sarcastic voice but Alexis seemed not to notice. He waved a slender, brown hand, like a young prince granting a pardon to one of his subjects. "Oh, it does not matter for once. I am good enough now to break my routine occasionally without any real harm. So you must not feel guilty."

"Oh. Oh, thank you very much," Charlie said.

Jo avoided his eyes. He would try to make her laugh—and she didn't want to laugh at Alexis. She said, to create a diversion, "Who was that, who opened the door to us?"

"Our maid, Phoebe. She has worked for my father's family since long before I was born. She looks after the house while we are in Zenith and when we wish to come here she makes everything ready. Now my mother is away, she takes care of me. She is devoted to me, of course."

"Oh, *of course*!" Charlie said.

Jo said quickly, "I only asked because I saw her talking to the policeman yesterday and I thought it seemed funny. Not many people in Polis will talk to him."

"Phoebe does what she likes, she is frightened of no one." His grey eyes shone brightly. "She is not an informer, if that is what you are thinking. She is not planted in our house as a spy! If the policeman were to do any harm to me, Phoebe would murder him! She is a strong, savage old woman."

Charlie said, in his silky, sarcastic voice, "What harm

could he do you?" Meaning—*who do you think you are, silly boy*!

Alexis looked perplexed. "He watches me. We have a landing stage down by the shore—we can reach it from our house by a stairway. The Government has confiscated our boat now but I have seen the policeman on the point by the lighthouse, watching through his binoculars in case someone comes secretly."

"Are you expecting someone?" Charlie asked innocently.

"Friends might come," Jo said. "Friends of his father's. Don't act *dumb*, Charlie."

Charlie raised his eyebrows. "I didn't think I was dumb. I may be quite wrong, of course, but I had the impression that I was talking. In fact, I think I am now. My tongue is moving and words are emerging from my mouth."

"Oh, very witty!" Jo turned to Alexis. "Come on, let's go. Leave my crazy brother to laugh at his own stupid jokes. Clever-Dick-Charlie!"

But Alexis was giggling. "He is very funny. I would like him to come with us." He smiled sweetly at Charlie. "Please do. We can go to the Citadel. I have things to show you and I know a quick way."

He led them through a network of lanes to the edge of the fortress, then ducked through an archway to a long, narrow tunnel that climbed vertically upwards. Rough steep steps were cut in the face of the rock. "Be careful," Alexis said. "You can break your ankle." He leapt ahead, like a goat, and they toiled, gasping, behind him. He waited by a narrow slit in the wall and said, "Do you need rest? I am not tired, but I am accustomed."

Charlie shook his head and Alexis laughed and bounded on lightly. Jo looked at Charlie's face, sweating with effort, and knew this was the wrong moment to ask him to be nice to Alexis. She said, all the same, "He doesn't mean to show off, he just wants us to like him. He doesn't see anything wrong in telling us the things he's good at."

Charlie snorted.

She said, "All that about how well he plays the violin is just what his parents have told him, and it's just natural to him to tell *us*."

Charlie groaned.

She said, "It's like offering someone a present when you want to be friends with them. Sweets or something the first day at a new school. Only he says, *look at me, aren't I clever and nice, won't you be friends with me*?

Charlie laughed, "Like a puppy? Bit old, isn't he? Though I don't mind that so much. What *burns* me is that nonsense about being watched all the time. As if he were really important. Perhaps his father is—we can always check that with Albert. Ask him if he's heard of Andreas Platonides. But a silly kid can't be."

"You're just jealous," Jo said. Whispered, rather—they had reached the end of their climb and she didn't want Alexis to hear. The tunnel snaked round the rock, in the sheer face below Santa Sophia, and came out above it in a tall, ruined watch tower. They climbed over a tumble of stones that had once framed a window and found Alexis outside, looking down at the Church. The Germans from the cruise ship straggling up the zig-zag path from the Lower Town. A white-haired man was running up and down the line, herding them like like a sheep dog. He rounded them up outside the Church door and they stood quiet while he lectured them, turning their heads to look where he pointed like obedient children.

"They won't bother us," Alexis said. "They are all too old to climb any higher."

They climbed up to the very top of the rock and down the other side to a small, gusty plateau where thin grasses streamed flat to the wind and withered weeds clattered. There were several pits here, their dark mouths almost hidden by thick, creeping plants. "The old cisterns," Alexis said. "They are very deep."

Charlie lay on his stomach and threw a stone into one of them. They heard it crash against the sides, down and down, echoing hollowly.

Alexis said, "You could hide an army up here. Guns and men."

Charlie sat up and looked round. From this windy eyrie they could see for miles; a wide sweep of bay and mountains beyond, range on blue range, the summits hidden in a long, dark, soft cloud like a pillow. The sun glinted through ragged slits at the edges and shone in bright, silver bars across the grey sea to the modern village on the mainland below them. Charlie sighed, green eyes narrowed and dreaming. "It would be a wonderful place to defend. No one could take you by surprise, not by sea, nor by land."

Alexis nodded, hugging his knees. "The people of Polis have always defended their city. They are good, honest men, not greedy or mean. My father says, one day we will sweep away all the badness, all the corruption and muddle in Zenith, and start afresh here with everything new. If Polis were the capital, Ithaca would be a great country again as it was in the old days."

Charlie said, "Once upon a time. I suppose talk doesn't cost much."

Alexis looked blank.

Charlie said, "I mean, your father's in exile. He can't do anything, can he?"

"Oh, but he can!" Alexis jumped up, face exultant. "I cannot explain to you how it will happen but it won't be long now. My father will come back with all the other good men. They will shoot the Dictator and everyone who has supported him, the Secret Police, and the Generals. There will be a blood bath and we will be clean again."

Charlie wrinkled his nose with distaste. His expression was incredulous and weary. He said, "God preserve us!"

Alexis looked at him, frowning. He turned to Jo and said, with hurt surprise, "Why does he not believe me?"

Although Jo didn't believe him either, she thought it was mean of Charlie not to pretend to. "Pay no attention," she said. "He's just grouchy and jealous because nothing exciting ever happens to him. He thinks you're just saying all this to make yourself seem important."

Charlie ignored this. "It just couldn't happen so easily. I mean, it's not possible. The Dictator has the Army behind him. He has tanks and guns."

"My father has the people," Alexis said proudly. "When my father comes, they will rally to him with joy. They will run through the streets weeping with happiness because he has brought them their freedom."

"After the blood bath, or before? The people your father is going to shoot will hardly be weeping with happiness, will they?"

"Perhaps he won't shoot them. Perhaps he'll just put them in prison on one of the islands."

"Make your mind up!"

Alexis flinched as if Charlie had struck him. He said in a sad, helpless voice, "I cannot tell what my father will do once he has power. All I know is that he *will* have it quite soon."

Charlie smiled; a brief, disbelieving, grim smile.

Alexis hunched his shoulders and stared at the ground. He looked so dejected, Jo was angry with Charlie. "You're a pig," she hissed at him. "A mean, rotten pig. It's just as I told you, he wants to be *friends*. Why can't you let him? I wish I'd not brought you."

Alone with Alexis, she thought, she could have pretended; it would have been fun, a good game. She said, "You always spoil everything."

"Sorry, I'm sure," Charlie said.

Alexis lifted his head. He said slowly, "Charlie . . . if I tell you something, a secret, will you believe me?"

Grey eyes met green ones. Charlie laughed. He said, "Try me."

Alexis said, "My father does not need tanks or planes. As I said, the people are for him. What I did not tell you, and this is the secret, is that the Navy is on his side, too. Next week, on our National Day, all our ships will be in the harbour at Zenith for the celebrations. The Dictator and the Generals will parade through the city, down to the water front, and go aboard the flag ship for the Salute of Nine Guns. This salute will be the signal for freedom. When the ninth gun is fired, the Admiral of the Fleet will arrest the Dictator. Even if some of the Army officers remain loyal to him, they will be helpless because the Navy will hold him as a hostage. My father will be in Zenith with all the other exiled politicians and they will take over the Government."

There was a silence. Charlie was watching Alexis with a curious expression. Finally he cleared his throat, blinked, and said, "Very neat."

Alexis said, "Do you believe me?"

To Jo's amazement, Charlie nodded.

Alexis laughed. "Then you are my friend now?"

"Oh yes," Charlie said. "Yes, of course."

They had a fine time after that. They shared the food Niki's grandmother had packed them for lunch—coarse bread, white cheese, sweet tomatoes—and scrambled over the rock until the sun disappeared and the rain came. Light and pleasant at first, prickling their hot skin with cold needles, it quickly grew heavier, pelting down from the dark sky and blowing across the rock in great sheets of water. None of the ruined towers offered much shelter and by the time they had climbed down to the Santa Sophia Church they were so wet there was no point in waiting there for the storm to be over. Alexis looked like a wet seal with his purple shirt clinging to his chest and his dark hair flat to his head. "Come tomorrow," he begged. "Please. I am so happy to have two new friends, there is so much I can show you."

He spoke to them both but it seemed to Jo it was Charlie he wanted. Another boy, not a stupid girl! She said, "We'll see when tomorrow comes," and ran off, feeling grumpy and jealous. Charlie caught her up but she squelched on in her soaking sandals, face averted. The wind and the rain blew in their faces as they trudged out of the town down the road round the rock to the harbour. As it came into view, they saw the German ship leaving, rolling in the steep waves and looking very low in the water.

Charlie said, "They'll be sea-sick. What's the matter?"

"Nothing."

"Aw, come on! Are you angry?"

She shook her head. What she felt was humiliating; she couldn't admit to it. She said, "I was only thinking.

Wondering what made you change suddenly. You didn't believe Alexis to start with."

"Nor to finish with, either. I was just suddenly sorry. I saw it was true what you'd said—he's lonely and he wants friends. I was sorry I'd pushed him into making a fool of himself with more lies."

"*Was* he lying?"

"Must have been, mustn't he?"

"You don't *know*!"

"Isn't it obvious? I mean, if his father is plotting something, some kind of takeover, which isn't impossible, he would hardly send a letter to Master Platonides giving him chapter and verse. And there's no other way he could know. I thought I might face him with it and then I thought, no, that's mean! The poor kid."

"He's almost as old as you are."

"Well, he's young for his age. He'd be bound to be, living that queer, shut-off life, wouldn't he? Left alone most of the time with that old woman for company and when his parents are there, petted and fussed and told he's a genius. No wonder he's a bit batty."

She said indignantly, "He's not batty!"

Charlie laughed. Rain flew off the end of his nose in bright drops as he laughed at her.

"Don't laugh at me! I hate that!"

He coughed, choked a bit, then stopped. "I know. I'm sorry. And while I'm about it, I'm sorry I laughed at Alexis too. You hated that too, didn't you?"

"A bit."

"A *lot*! I would have done in your place." He looked thoughtful. "I wonder . . ."

"Wonder what?"

Turning the last bend they came on to the causeway out of the little shelter the rock had provided and the wind blew them sideways. It caught Charlie's voice and tossed it away. She heard two words only. ". . . ask Albert."

She screamed, "*No*!" and clutched Charlie. He put his arm round her, to steady her, and they staggered like a pair of drunks over the causeway. He bellowed, close to her ear, "I just thought, we could ask him about Andreas Platonides. Whether there could be any truth in it. In what Alexis was saying . . ."

She saved her breath until they had reached the village. They stopped to rest in the lee of the first house. They were drenched and gasping. She said, "Please, Charlie. I don't want to ask Albert *anything*. Not about Alexis, or his father, or anything else in the world just at the moment . . ."

Chapter 7

She thought she would never be able to meet Albert's eye, let alone ask him questions! *A traitor*, she had called him, *a coward*. If someone had called her those names she would hate them for ever.

Lying on her bed, reading an Agatha Christie, she heard them come back. Alice and James banging up the stairs, shouting; Carrie and Albert talking and laughing and then greeting Charlie who came out of his room to ask them if they'd had a good day. Jo put the Agatha Christie under her pillow and opened the selected poems of W. B. Yeats that Albert had given her. She read slowly, aloud, "*I know that I shall meet my fate somewhere among the clouds above, Those that I fight I do not hate, those that I guard I do not love.*"

A terrible sadness caught her throat; tears made the print wobble and dance. Alice burst in and jumped on the bed, up and down on her knees, making the wooden slats groan under the mattress. "We've been on a picnic, a picnic," she chanted, "and there was a big storm, a *big* storm, and Albert picked me up and we ran to the car . . ."

"*My country is Kiltartan Cross, my countrymen Kiltartan's*

poor, No likely end could bring them loss, Or leave them happier than before," Jo read, lifting her voice so Albert could hear her. "*Nor law, nor duty bade me fight, Nor public men, nor cheering crowds . . .*"

"*A lonely impulse of delight,*" Albert said, from the doorway, "*Drove to this tumult in the clouds.* One of my favourites, Jo, I'm glad you like it." He smiled and vanished before she could finish the poem but she felt more comfortable. At least he had spoken to her, not turned from her with loathing. She wouldn't have to pretend she felt too sick to eat. She could go down to dinner and behave as if nothing had happened.

She couldn't quite manage that. She took the book of poems with her and put it open beside her plate. Although they were not allowed to read at the table, neither Carrie nor Albert said anything, and after a bit this made her feel worse, not better. She had the feeling that if she looked up from her book she would find they were watching her anxiously as if she were a dangerous dog that might jump up and bite them. She imagined what they had said to each other. "We can't have another public scene like that one at breakfast. You know what she's like, so sudden and violent . . ."

She felt hot with despair. Of course they hated her. They were right to. She hated herself. She was vile. She tried to look up, to smile and be ordinary, but did not dare raise her eyes higher than Alice and James who were too young to understand how hateful she was. She said loudly, "Do you think we'll be able to swim again, Alice? I'd like to, if the weather gets better tomorrow."

Alice looked surprised. "That's what we've been talking about. Weren't you listening? We're going to the long beach, a new place we've not been to. Albert says it's safer there when the sea's rough and blowy."

They went to this beach in the morning, walking along the road from the hotel for about half a mile, then turning down to the shore through a belt of little farms and scrub land. The earth was dry as dust between the rows of thin, standing corn, and the few farmers they passed looked at them sourly. "They're very poor here," Albert said.

"Would they be richer if someone got rid of the Dictator?" Charlie asked—apparently out of the blue, but Jo knew he was thinking of Alexis's father.

"Not really," Albert said. "When you're at the bottom of the heap, it doesn't make too much difference who's at the top." He glanced at Jo. "Like the Kiltartan poor in that poem of Yeats. *No likely end can bring them loss, or leave them happier than before.*"

He smiled at her, so did Carrie. Their kind smiles seemed false and forced to her. They had been talking her over and planned to be kind! She sighed and wriggled her shoulders and ran on, to the sea.

The beach was made up of multi-coloured pebbles, so small that walking on them was like walking on rough, gritty sand. She stood at the edge of the water and the waves broke and curled round her ankles, hissing with these tiny, bright stones.

It was warm enough to swim, but too rough for Alice to use her inflatable duck. "As long as you're careful and stay close to the shore," Carrie said, when Jo asked if she might. Jo had the feeling her mother would have liked to say no but was afraid of offending her. She said, "I'll be careful, I promise."

The sea was warm and soupy with the sand and small stones the storm had churned up. Jo clung to the duck's rubber neck and lay on her back, legs trailing out. Grey and black clouds raced above her and she saw people in them; fat cheeks, bulbous noses, great billowing stomachs. A gull swooped down and settled quite close to her; its cold, yellow eye accepted her as another sea creature. She said, "Hallo, Mister Gull," and laughed as the swell lifted her and dropped her into a hollow. When she rose on the next wave the gull had gone.

She looked at the shore and it seemed miles away. James was splashing about at the edge of the water. Carrie and Charlie were setting up the canvas windbreak and Albert and Alice were collecting stones. They looked like birds walking; a tall, pale, skinny bird and a smaller, black one. Jo saw Alice crouch down and then run to Albert, holding her hand out.

She realised she was moving fast through the water without any effort. She reared her head and saw that the tail of the duck had risen up in the wind and was acting like a sail, blowing her. She shifted her grasp towards the duck's middle but this only made its tail lift up higher. The wind was as strong as a wall and she could do nothing against it. She put her feet down but she was out of her depth and there was nothing beneath her. She thought of sharks, down in those murky depths, cruel mouths smiling, and drew her legs up.

Too scared to try and swim in case the sharks saw her legs moving, she let go the duck with one arm and waved frantically. Someone must see her! She could see *them*! Any second now, they would start shouting and screaming and rush to her rescue.

But they all went peacefully on with what they were doing. No one looked seaward, so there was no point in waving. She thought bitterly—*Serve them right if I drown!*—and for perhaps thirty seconds, drowned was what she wanted to be, to teach them a lesson. Drowned, she would be no more trouble to anyone. They would deal out her things, books for Charlie, good clothes set aside for Alice when she was older, and then forget she ever existed. They would be happy without her! She gasped, and the salt sea rushed into her mouth and down her throat, choking her. She went under the water, fought her way up, coughing and spluttering—and knew she didn't want to drown after all. She yelled into the wind, "Help me, please, help . . ." and, like a miracle, a voice answered her.

"*Keep shouting.*" She hauled herself up on the duck with

what felt like the last of her strength and saw Albert's head bobbing towards her. "Here," she called, "*here*"—and started swimming towards him.

They bumped together; his strong arm went round her. He said, "Little fool, why didn't you swim before? I thought you must have got cramp. There's no current, only the duck blowing you out, why didn't you let it go?"

She wailed sadly, "I couldn't lose Alice's duck!"

"Idiot!" Albert said. Without his glasses, his face was a stranger's face, naked and angry. He yanked the duck round and pushed it towards the shore, dragging her with it. She kicked her legs, helping him. As they drew near the beach, Carrie and Charlie ran into the water. Charlie took the duck from her and she staggered and rolled in the shallows, the shingle tingling and burning all over her. Carrie seized her arm painfully, pulling her up. She said, "Darling, are you all right?"—but she was talking to Albert. He was half-sitting, half-lying at the edge of the water, goose-pimpled and shivering. Carrie knelt beside him and rubbed his hands. She said, "Charlie, get a towel and his glasses." She looked at Jo. "Why do you never pay any attention? I told you not to go out too far but you're always the same, you always know best. I suppose it's too much to hope you've learned a lesson this time. You could both have drowned."

Perhaps she was only angry and frightened but Jo saw dreadful things in her face.

She said, "If it had been just me, you wouldn't have minded."

Albert was struggling to his feet. His breath rattled in and out of his chest. He wheezed, "Jo . . ." but she stormed off to the windbreak. Her legs shook beneath her, there was a huge, empty hollow where her stomach should be, her hands were cramped and cold, just like Albert's, but no one cared about her, of course! She tugged her jeans on over her wet bathing suit, moaning, "I wish I was dead, I wish I was dead, I wish I was dead," all on one note, like a litany. Alice stood there, round-eyed, and Jo turned on her. "I saved your duck. I don't suppose you'd think to say thank you." Alice's eyes grew bigger still, showing a lot of white, and this scared look made Jo want to hurt her. "I don't suppose you'd mind if I drowned, just as long as your old duck was safe, would you?"

Having said this, she felt better. A bit mean, but better. As she ran off, through the scrubland up to the road, she thought it was rather as if she'd been sick and got rid of some poison inside her. Carrie and Albert would make it all right with Alice, she knew. "*Poor Jo,*" they would say. "*Poor Jo, she didn't mean to be nasty, she was upset and frightened.*"

She laughed to herself as she skipped down the road, her clothes drying on her; dry, sticky salt rubbing her skin. When she reached the hotel and went up to change, she found red marks on her stomach and thighs where the small stones had scratched her. She washed in cold water, put on on her best denim skirt and green blouse and tied her wet hair with a ribbon. Looking at herself in the glass, she thought she was really quite pretty; she smiled and her reflection smiled sweetly back. Downstairs, she smiled in the same way at Niki who was setting tables for lunch, and said, "When the others come back will you tell them I've gone to the Lower Town? I'll get some lunch there, I've got enough money."

She wondered if Niki would offer to take her up to the rock on the back of his scooter but she wasn't hurt when he didn't. She was all right alone; free and happy. "One's family can be a nuisance, sometimes," she planned to say to Alexis. "One needs to be by oneself occasionally. I like Charlie, but he always thinks he knows everything and that can be tiresome."

Once she reached the town, though, she was too shy to call for Alexis. She hung round his house for a little, half-hoping he would come out by chance and find her, but the heavy door remained closed and the small windows that looked on the street were shuttered as if no one lived there. Jo thought —*I'll count to a hundred and then pull the bell*—but when she had counted, she hadn't the courage. It would be more polite, she decided, to have her lunch first in case it looked as if she had invited herself at this time for a meal. At the café in the main square she went to the kitchen to choose the fish she wanted to eat and then sat outside while it was cooked, putting her purse on the table to show she had enough money to pay. The fish, when it came, was full of small bones; she washed it down with several bottles of lemonade, filled up with bread, and felt full and sleepy. She climbed to the square where the old fig tree grew and settled in a corner to wait for Alexis. A line of brown ants marched in front of her, carrying bits of grass and seed pods like a foraging army and she teased them, trying to break the line and turn them aside with a stick, until her eyelids grew heavy. Although the wind howled and thumped through the old, gutted houses that surrounded the square, it was sheltered where she sat by the wall. If she went to sleep there, perhaps Alexis would come and find her. She arranged herself as gracefully as she could against the hard stone and thought, *a sleeping princess with red hair. . .*

When she woke, her mouth was dry and tasted of the fish she had eaten. No sign of Alexis. Only Alice, sitting on the wall and watching her gravely. "I thought you'd never wake up. I've been waiting and waiting."

Jo got up stiffly, sucking spit from the sides of her mouth to moisten her dry lips and tongue. "How'd you get here?"

"I came looking to find you."

"By yourself?"

"They all went up to look at the Church but I said I was tired." Her large eyes grew solemn. "I wanted to find you to say I was sorry."

"What for?"

"For not saying thank you for saving my duck." She hung her head sadly.

Jo grabbed her and hugged her. "You darling!" She felt

choked up; full to bursting. "I'm the one that should be sorry. I didn't mean what I said."

"Albert said that." The little girl put her arm round Jo's neck and squeezed fiercely. "I do love you," she whispered.

"Don't," Jo said. "I can't bear it."

Alice was so precious, so good and sweet, it wasn't enough just to love her. Jo wanted to give her something but nothing seemed good enough. She said, "Would you like an ice? Or a lemonade?"

Alice nodded. She hunched her shoulders up and looked shy.

"Come on, then." Jo took her small hand and they walked slowly together across the quiet square. Jo said, "This is where I met my friend Alexis, by that old tree. Do you see that bell? It used to be the school bell but the children all went away and now no one rings it except to warn the town people when something terrible happens. A fire, or a war, or something like that, so they can escape up the rock and hide from the danger. There's hundreds of places to hide up there in the Citadel. Old towers and deep wells. Alexis says you could hide an army up there. He says, one day the people of Polis will rise up against the Dictator and shoot him. That's the sort of thing boys always think of. Armies and fighting."

"Could you hide yourself up there if you'd done something bad?" Alice said.

"Like what? Like stealing a bride's necklace?" Jo asked,

teasing her. Last year, this had been the worst crime Alice could think of.

Alice shook her black pig-tails. She said, very husky and low, "If you'd killed someone. Could you run and hide there so no one could find you."

"Do you often want to kill people?"

"Sometimes." Alice's hand tightened in Jo's. "At school, sometimes, I want to kill my teacher. When she says I'm not writing nicely or I've spelled a word wrong." She looked up, her face creased and anxious. "Once I said, that's the way that *I* spell that word and my teacher laughed and I wanted to kill her."

Jo almost laughed too. Then she remembered. It was a long time since she had been as little as Alice, but she could remember wanting to murder people—usually other girls who had laughed at her or given away a secret she'd told them—and the feeling had frightened her. She had never dared tell anyone in case they should send her to prison.

She said carefully, "Wanting to do something, or saying you want to, isn't the same thing as doing it. I know it feels scary and I used to get scared about it when I was your age, wondering what would happen to me and thinking I must be dreadfully wicked, but I've never killed anyone, have I? And I stopped wanting to after a bit."

"Will I stop?"

"By the time you're about eight and a half, I should think."

"I'm nearly eight now."

"So the feeling should start wearing off pretty soon."

Alice smiled. The smile spread over her face. She said, "Thank you, Jo." As if she'd been given a present.

Jo said, "Everyone grows out of it. I should think most people want to kill other people when they're young, some time or other. I expect even Albert did!"

But Alice had heard enough. She let go Jo's hand and ran ahead down a short flight of steps. At the bottom she turned and looked back. "Which way now?"

"I'm not sure."

Talking, they had missed the way to the square and come lower down the Old Town than they had been before, to a maze of covered lanes all of which seemed to lead further down still. They tried one, and it came to a dead end in what looked as if it had once been a garden but was now a dump for rubbish; neglected trees and shrubs straggled up through heaps of sour garbage. They went back and tried the next opening, a low, slimy-walled tunnel. "I can smell sea," Alice said, and the tunnel curved round and brought them out on to rocks with spray flying. Along to their right was a concrete platform with iron rings set into it and a rusty ladder that went down into the water. At that moment an old woman came out of a rough doorway in the face of the rock carrying a basket of washing. The maid, Phoebe. Old Brown-Teeth.

She didn't see them. She went to the far edge of the platform, knelt down, and started slapping white sheets and towels in and out of the water.

"I know where we are, I think," Jo whispered to Alice. "It's the landing stage where Alexis and his family used to keep their boat. There must be a way up through that door."

"Come on, then," Alice said.

"We can't. It's a *house*."

"It doesn't say Private." Alice giggled. "Quick, while she's busy."

She nipped across the platform and into the doorway. Following, Jo couldn't see her, only hear her feet clattering up. Stone steps went round and round like a staircase in a tower. Little lamps, set in holes in the wall, gave enough light to see and, at the top, in what seemed a cellar, full of barrels and sacks, pale sun filtered in through a dusty, barred window. No way out, they thought to begin with; then saw a low door in the corner. It creaked as they opened it. There were more steps beyond.

It was Alice's turn to hang back. Perhaps the door creaking had frightened her. "Someone might hear us. It's like being burglars."

"It's all right. I know Alexis. He's my friend. We've only come visiting."

Alice's mouth turned down at the corners. "It's not like an ordinary house. It's not like going visiting through someone's back door. It's like creeping into an ogre's castle."

"You wanted to come. You said it didn't say Private!"

"It *feels* Private now!" Alice's eyes rolled white with fear. "Let's go back down."

"We might meet Brown-Teeth coming up. That old woman. She doesn't speak English so we couldn't explain. We've got to go on. Don't worry, no one will hurt you."

She pretended to be braver than she felt, to comfort Alice, and it was a relief, as she turned the next bend in the stairway, to hear music. Someone was playing a piano; a soft, sweeping, rather sad tune.

She thought—*Alexis*! Alexis practising to be a genius. She laughed inside herself and ran on tip-toe up the last of the steps and pushed at a half-open door.

Light struck her eyes, dazzling her. Someone said, "What are you doing here?"

Not Alexis—but the voice was familiar. Jo blinked, and the room she stood in took shape; a long, beautiful room with a shining, wood floor and bright rugs hanging on walls of pale stone. There was a grand piano at the far end. The man who had spoken rose from behind it and came forward to meet them.

It was Herr Schmidt. His bald head gleamed in the light from the window. He said, in an astonished voice, "How did you get in?"

"We came up from the sea . . ." Jo began, and then closed her mouth firmly. This wasn't Herr Schmidt's house; it wasn't his business to question her.

"It was my fault," Alice said mournfully. "I said it didn't say Private." She clung to the back of Jo's skirt and peeped round.

Jo said boldly, "We came to visit my friend, Alexis. He lives here. We didn't expect to see you."

"No," Herr Schmidt said. "I imagine not. . ."

He stopped. There were steps—running steps—on the stairs. Alexis burst in, flushed and eager. He said, "Father. . ." Then he saw Jo and his hand flew to his mouth. "Oh," he said. "*Oh*!"

For a few seconds no one moved or spoke. It was as if a spell held them.

Then Herr Schmidt said, with a rueful laugh, "Oh Alexis, Alexis!" and the spell was broken

Alexis hung his head miserably. Jo let out her breath in a sigh and Alice came out from hiding behind her. She gazed at Herr Schmidt with round, startled eyes and Herr Schmidt smiled back at her.

He said, "Since my son has given the secret away, I had better introduce myself. I am Andreas Platonides."

Chapter 8

"But you can't be," Jo said. "I mean, Herr Schmidt's such. . ." She stopped and laughed awkwardly. She had been going to say, "such a horrible person," but it seemed rude, somehow.

"Such an unpleasant man?" Andreas Platonides said. "I agree with you. I dislike him more and more the longer I have to live with him. But it would not be a good idea if he were too agreeable because people might wish to be friendly with him and that could make difficulties. Not only because it is hard to be unpleasant consistently if it is not your true nature, but because my German is not as good as it would be if I were really Herr Schmidt from Hamburg. I can speak well enough for most practical purposes but I would find it hard to deceive someone who spoke really fluently."

"That's why you didn't want to talk to the Germans from the cruise ship?"

"Precisely."

Andreas Platonides smiled and Jo felt confused. He didn't sound like Herr Schmidt any longer but he still looked like him and that was disturbing. As if there were two people inside the same body: Andreas, who spoke, and Herr Schmidt, who stood smiling.

Alexis said, "My father is a wonderful actor. He is very clever and cunning." He took a framed photograph from a table and showed her. Jo looked from the dark haired, clean shaven man in the picture, to the bald, bearded one smiling at her, and the person she had known as Herr Schmidt seemed to dissolve and disappear like a reflection in water when the wind blows it. Alexis said, "My father has to shave his head twice a day because his hair grows so quickly."

"A simple trick, but effective," Andreas said. "People look at the bald head and the beard and forget the face in between."

"*I* knew you at once!" Alexis said. He went to his father and leaned against him.

"Ah, but you are a wise child! A genius!" Although Andreas laughed, this seemed only partly a joke. He put his arm round his son and looked at him with such open love that Jo was embarrassed and jealous.

She said, impatiently, "Anyone who really knew you would know who you were." Niki knew, she was sure of it! That sly, teasing look when he had asked Herr Schmidt to interpret for the cruise party. And there was something else; a vague memory nudging the edge of her mind that slipped away when she chased it. She said, "People round here. I mean, they must know you."

"No one in Polis would betray my father," Alexis said proudly.

Jo thought how he had betrayed him, the lies he had told her and Charlie, and looked at him, hard. She was pleased to see him turn white.

He stammered, "Oh, Father, I'm sorry. I shouldn't have talked to her. But I have no friends here and I was so lonely."

Andreas said gently, "It is all right, Alexis. I think no great harm has been done. The little girl is too young to understand, and since Jo is your friend, I trust her as I trust you. She is an intelligent girl and you will explain to her that my visit is private. That I have only come to see my dear son." He bowed to Jo, gravely and courteously. "I apologise for my deception but there is a good reason for it. Perhaps we will meet again in happier circumstances, and it will be my pleasure to entertain you and the rest of your family."

Jo's heart swelled proudly. Andreas Platonides had said that he trusted her! He was so calm and dignified, she could see why the people of Ithaca might want him to rule them. She wanted to say something polite, something that would fit this occasion, but she couldn't think what. She smiled and said, "Thank you."

Alexis led them out of the beautiful room. At a bend in the stairway, a short passage took them into a square, gloomy hall lit by a small lamp and smelling of polish and flowers. A great bowl of lilies stood on a carved, shining, oak chest, and, for some reason, their sweet, heavy scent made Jo feel uneasy. There was something she knew, something she ought to remember . . . Then Alexis opened the door to the street and the fresh air streamed in.

"I know where we are now!" Alice said in a loud, relieved voice. "The café's up that way. In the big square. Mum and Albert said, when they'd been to the Church, they'd wait for us there."

Her little face that had been pinched up and solemn, smoothed out with smiles. "*I* wasn't frightened of ogres!" she announced, to the air, and stumped off, up the steps. Jo called after her, "Alice, wait . . ." but the child didn't hear her.

Alexis said, "Let her go. There is an English proverb I have learned. Least said, soonest mended." He was leaning against the wall of the house, his eyes closed. He looked drained and exhausted. He went on in a low voice, "Thank you for not telling my father what I told you and Charlie. I should not have told you. If he knew, he would never forgive me."

Jo said contemptuously, "All those *lies*!"

His grey eyes snapped open.

She said, "Well, they were, weren't they? All that about plots and blood baths and taking over the Government! If I were you, I'd be ashamed! Telling lies like that about my own father!"

She saw that his eyes were bewildered. For a second, doubt flicked her.

She said, "I mean, if they were true . . ." She thought of what Charlie had said and laughed coldly. "I mean, if your father had really planned to get rid of the Dictator, he'd hardly come here, just to tell you!"

Alexis said slowly, "He wanted to see me. He was afraid it could be the last time. If something went wrong." He hesitated. "He loves me."

Jo tossed her head. "No one loves children that much! Not enough to risk something important. You were just showing off. Boasting, to make yourself big. You're just a silly kid, Charlie says, and you're young for your age."

This was the worst insult she could think of. She stepped back in case he got angry and hit her. But he stayed where he was, limply leaning against the house wall, and she saw his throat move as he swallowed.

At last he said, "My father does not think that."

"Oh, I know! He thinks you're a genius!"

"Not quite, that is a bit of a joke, but he does believe I am exceptionally clever." Alexis sighed, as if the weight of this was too much for him. "My father thinks I cannot be like other boys because I am his son and that makes me special. He trusts me." He caught his breath and tears sprang to his eyes. "Oh," he said. "I wish I was dead."

He looked so unhappy she wanted to comfort him. She said, "Don't be silly. You didn't give him away. I mean, you told Charlie and me *about* him, but never once said he was here, in disguise. I found that out for myself, didn't I? Bursting in, me and Alice . . ."

She thought about that for a minute; about how Herr Schmidt had changed before her eyes into Andreas Platonides and how strange it had seemed. As if people were only what they told you they were; as if what you *saw* didn't matter.

She said, "He didn't seem to mind all that much, either. If he'd really had something to hide, apart from just being here, he would have been scared, wouldn't he? I mean, if there really had been that *plot* you were on about, he'd have been scared we might give it away. He'd have done something! Locked us up, so we couldn't say anything. Who could have stopped him?"

Alexis said wearily, "That would have made much more trouble. Your parents would have come looking for you and Charlie would know that you might be with me. There was nothing my father could do except make light of it all and let you go and hope that you will not tell anyone because there is not much to tell. Just that he is here on a visit, and to you and your family that cannot be very important."

"It could be, to Alice. She may not understand about politics but she does understand about fathers and families. Suppose she points at Herr Schmidt this evening while we're having dinner and shouts, *That's not Herr Schmidt, that's Alexis's Daddy*!"

She started to laugh as she pictured this scene, Alice pointing and shouting in her shrill treble and everyone turning to look, Albert and Carrie and Niki. But of course, Niki knew! That first night, she had heard him talking to Albert and saying, "He came for the boy . . ."

Alexis was smiling. "Then you would have to stop her. But it cannot happen. My father . . ."

She said, amazed, "Albert knows who he is! He's known all along!"

"Not so loud." Alexis put his finger to his lips and looked nervously round him.

Jo said, "I must talk to Albert," and started up the steps to the square.

Alexis ran after her. "Wait a minute. . ." He caught her up and clutched her arm. "Don't go yet. Look. You can't talk to him now."

The square was crowded as it always was in the early evening; children playing and shouting and people sitting outside the café. Carrie and Albert saw her and waved and she waved back self-consciously. She had been so stupid this morning, running off from the beach like an angry baby! She blushed as she thought about it; she sat on the sea wall, turning her face to the cool, healing wind and said, "Look at that *huge* black cloud. Is there going to be a storm, do you think?"

"I hope not." Alexis looked at the sky and the heaving sea, then at her. "My father is leaving tonight. When it is dark, a boat will come for him." He bit his lip and said anxiously, "I have to tell you this so you will know there is no danger from your little sister. But you must not repeat it to anyone."

She shook her head and he looked at her sadly. "Even if you do not believe me, you will keep it a secret?"

"I believe you about the boat," she said. She felt sorry she had been so mean to him earlier. "I'd have believed all the other things if it wasn't for Charlie. He's a very disbelieving sort of person, I'm afraid."

He didn't reply to this, only sighed. Then he plucked a blue flower that was growing out of a crack in the wall and gave it to her. He said, "As blue as your eyes."

She was pleased—and embarrassed. She said, "My eyes are hazel, really," and poked the stem of the flower through her shirt button hole.

Someone said, "Oh, isn't that *darling*!"

They turned, startled. Miss Emmeline and Miss Ottoline Skinner were smiling at them. Miss Ottoline was pointing a camera.

She said, "That was a charming shot. Do you mind if I take another? The colour, you know! That dark sky and your lovely, red hair."

Alexis moved away, grinning. Jo sat, feeling foolish. The camera clicked. Miss Ottoline said, "If you'd turn your chin just a little? That's perfect, dear. You have beautiful cheekbones."

Behind them, Alexis stuck his thumb up in agreement and laughed.

Miss Ottoline said, in her soft, drawly voice, "Now, honey, if I could have just one with a smile?"

Jo bared her teeth, watching Alexis who was running across the square. At the top of the steps he turned to wave; then his dark head bobbed down out of sight.

"That's fine, really fine," Miss Ottoline said. "When we're back home, I'll send you a print."

"When are you going home?" Jo asked politely.

Miss Emmeline said, "We're off to Zenith the day after tomorrow. We've scheduled our trip to be back in the city in time for the National Day. Tilly should get some fine pictures of the parade and I plan to do a political piece for the paper."

Jo sat still on the wall. She felt her face going stiff. She said, through stiff lips, "The Salute of Nine Guns."

"I believe there is some such ceremony," Miss Emmeline said, "I shall read up about it beforehand, of course. Celebrations in these small countries are so quaint and colourful. Rooted in history."

"When is it, exactly?"

Miss Ottoline said, "On Monday, isn't it, Emmy? I know we allowed ourselves a clear week-end to get there. Plenty of camera time in the mountains."

"Tilly can't bear to pass a good view," Miss Emmeline said indulgently.

"No," Jo said. "No, of course not."

She got down from the wall. Both ladies beamed at her toothily.

Miss Emmeline said, "Perhaps your family will pose for Tilly before we leave. A group picture for our private scrap book. We've been so happy here. It's such a peaceful place that it is hard to realise the country is under the yoke of a tyrant. The people seem so calm and content."

"Mr Sandwich says that Niki's father is in prison," Miss Ottoline reminded her.

"I haven't forgotten that, Tilly!" Miss Emmeline bridled slightly as if she thought this side of things was her business and her cousin should stick to taking her pictures! "But one mustn't judge hastily, nor altogether on what other people have told us. Even someone as well-informed as Mr Sandwich may have a biased view! I admit I came here with strong feelings about the Dictator, it's natural for an American to dislike authoritarian Governments, but all I can honestly do when I go home is report what I have seen for myself, and what I have seen so far is an ordered and pleasant country. No violence, no petty crime! No need to fear for your cameras, Tilly! People don't steal here."

Miss Ottoline's colour rose. She stretched her giraffe's neck. "My cameras are not the only thing I care about, Emmy."

"I know, dear. And I am as concerned as you are about Niki's father. As I would be concerned for anyone in prison unjustly. I am simply trying to keep my mind open. Not let my imagination run away with me." Miss Emmeline Skinner laughed, deep in her throat. "I find that pretty hard work sometimes."

She looked at her cousin as if she expected her to laugh too, but Miss Ottoline said, gently and obstinately, "Perhaps being in Zenith on the National Day will remind you of what is really going on here. The soldiers, the marching—the Iron Fist, Emmy!"

They wandered off, arguing. Jo felt very strange, confused and excited. Her mind was like a jigsaw, she thought;

a jumble of pieces. What she'd seen and heard, what Alexis had told her, what Charlie had said. The kind of jigsaw that needs time and patience. She thought—*I'll ask Albert to help me.* Charlie had said they should ask him about Andreas Platonides but she hadn't wanted to. She had said, *I don't want to ask Albert anything*! Well, she did now. Later this evening, when she could get him alone, she would tell him everything. Or tomorrow perhaps, would be better. There was no hurry. She had promised Alexis she would say nothing about the boat but by tomorrow his father would be safely away, out of danger.

She felt light with relief. She ran across the square and her family looked up and smiled at her welcomingly. Albert and Carrie and Charlie and James—all smiling as if they had missed her. She smiled back at them happily and said, "Hi, there! Can I have a drink too? I had fish for lunch and I'm thirsty. I'd have come before but I was talking to my friend Alexis. Where's Alice? Didn't she find you?"

Albert turned in his chair. Jo looked where he looked and one piece of the jigsaw that had been floating about in her mind fell into place. She knew why the smell of lilies in Alexis's house had made her uneasy; knew what it was she should have remembered.

On a bench against the wall of the café, Alice was sitting on the fat policeman's knee.

Chapter 9

She said nothing to no one. Nothing to Albert, nothing to Charlie. Nothing, even, to Alice. What good would it do? Alice must have seen her on the sea wall with Alexis. It was too much to hope that she had not told the fat policeman. *That's my sister's friend, Alexis, and I've just seen his Daddy.*

Jo hoped, all the same. A mixture of hope and fear kept her silent. She recognised the feeling as one she had often had when she was little and done something bad. If she said nothing, did nothing, pretended to herself hard enough that nothing had happened, it would be as if nothing had. No one would find out, leap on her to punish her. Danger would recede and fade like a nightmare in daylight . . .

And it seemed to. They finished their drinks, drove back to the hotel, washed and changed, went down for dinner. Herr Schmidt was not there but Miss Emmeline and Miss Ottoline were already eating and waved at them cheerfully, showing their fine, glossy teeth. Tables were set inside the restaurant because the wind had got up; by the end of the meal it was blowing so hard that one of the doors to the terrace cracked open and a glass panel shattered. Charlie helped Niki fasten the door back and clear up the mess and Alice coaxed the hotel cats into a corner with morsels of fish so they wouldn't cut their feet on the glass. Thunder rolled round the sky like steel balls in a great bowling alley, white lightning split the black sky over the rock and Miss Ottoline Skinner rushed to her room to take photographs from the balcony. Carrie said James could sleep in her bed because he was frightened and Jo said kindly to Alice, "You can sleep in mine if you want to," thinking it would be comfortable to have her to cuddle.

"I'm not scared," Alice said smugly. "I'm scared of witches and ogres and dungeons and swishing down the plug hole with the bath water but I'm not frightened of thunder."

"Bed then, my brave girl," Albert said, and swung her up on his shoulder.

A bit later on, he came to say goodnight and read Alice a story. He read her "The Goose Girl". She knew it so well that she murmured the words after him until her eyes closed. She was fast asleep by the time he had finished. He tucked the blankets up round her ears and went to the windows to make sure the shutters were fastened. The window slammed against them like a gun firing. "Pity the poor sailors," Albert said.

Jo almost told him then. But she was afraid it would come out muddled and silly. She couldn't make good, clear sense of all that she knew in her own mind, so how could she explain it to Albert? What could Albert do, anyway? If he did try to do something, warn Andreas Platonides, he might get into danger himself. A new and sharper dread seized her. Albert was a criminal already, bringing those letters in! Alexis had said so. He had said they could send him to prison! Jo watched Albert struggling with an iron bar that refused to slip into its slot, and thought, *He keeps us safe, I must keep him safe, too*! When he turned from the window, pushing his glasses up on his nose, she laughed and said, "What a storm!"

It went on all through the night. In the morning, although the thunder and lightning had stopped, the wind was still high and the sea hissed and boiled, turning the clear rocky pool where they usually swam into a bubbling cauldron of ink. The only thing was a picnic inland, Albert said, and asked Niki's grandmother to provide a packed lunch. Jo put on an act of yawning and sleepiness. "I'd rather stay if you don't mind," she said, and Charlie said he thought he'd stay too. When the others had gone, they strolled down the road to the harbour and he looked at her doubtfully. "Is anything wrong? You seem a bit—I don't know—*funny*."

"Ha, ha."

"No, stupid. Not that."

"I'm sure I don't know what you mean, then. Why should there be anything wrong?"

"I was asking you that."

She sighed heavily. "It's just I hate picnics."

"That s not true, is it? I mean you never *have*. Not before."

"Well, I've changed. A person can change, can't they? There's no law against it."

"Not that I know of." But he was still watching her.

She said, "I just wanted to stay. I thought I might want to go up to the rock."

"Oh, I see." He grinned knowingly.

"No you don't, Clever-Dick-Charlie! All I thought was, it might be nice to explore a bit without the others tailing along. We could climb up to the Citadel."

"In this weather? We'd be blown off like paper."

"The wind might ease off. I like the wind, anyway." She staggered along the road, arms spread like wings. Then she whirled round and danced backwards and her hair flew over her face. "It's *wild*, isn't it? Do you think a boat could take off in this weather?"

"Depends what sort of boat. None of the fishing boats went out this morning."

The harbour was full of them; small, brightly coloured boats with huge eyes painted on them.

"Against the perils of the deep," Charlie said. "I wonder if it does protect them."

"Just superstition. Like St Christopher medals."

"You can't *know*," Charlie said. "I mean, you can't prove it."

They leaned on the harbour wall, looking down at a shoal of fish in the brown, sheltered water. From time to time they flashed silver as the light caught them.

"I suppose you'd be safe in a large boat," Jo said. She looked out to sea and thought it seemed calmer.

Charlie laughed and she turned on him. "What's *that* for?"

"Nothing. Just you! Bursting with something, it sticks out a mile. If you want to tell me, I'll listen. Till you do, I'm going to sit here and read."

He settled down comfortably against a thick coil of rope and took a paperback out of his pocket. Jo waited a bit but he refused to look up and she wandered off restlessly. She walked round the harbour, stood for a while watching the fishermen mending their nets, then walked back again, very slowly. Charlie was where she had left him, still steadily reading. She perched on the harbour wall, watching the gulls wheel and dip and listening to the lazy creak of the boats as they moved in the water. She thought of what Alice said sometimes. *I'm getting bored, waiting.*

What was she waiting for? She knew what she ought to do. She ought to go to the Lower Town and find Alexis. Whether his father was still there or not, he ought to know about the policeman and Alice.

Ought, ought, she thought. *No "ought" about it.* No one would know if she simply did nothing. She could sit here the rest of the day with the boats and the gulls and Charlie slumped over his book and no one would blame her because no one know what she knew. She needn't blame herself either. She hadn't asked Alice what she had told her fat friend, only guessed. *Why* hadn't she asked her?

She started to yawn. She yawned till her eyes stung with

tears. *Scared*, she thought scornfully, remembering how she always yawned at the dentist's. She said, aloud, "Well, then, better get on with it!"

"Get on with what?" Charlie asked. He looked up, eyes narrowed into green slits. He looked at her, then beyond her. His eyes widened. He sprang up and started to run.

A harsh, rattling sound filled the air. A helicopter came round the rock, flying low, and hovered over the causeway. Jo ran after Charlie, towards it; the fishermen ran, and the women and children. The helicopter landed in a cloud of red dust, a whirlwind of grit that held the crowd back. They stood in a rough circle, staring and coughing. "What the hell?" Charlie said.

Soldiers jumped from the aircraft, rifles slung from their backs. The villagers watched them in silence. A child shouted something and its mother shook it and slapped it. The soldiers looked round at them, grinning.

Jo whispered, "Alexis." Charlie turned his head sharply. She spat dust and groaned. "His father . . ."

Miraculously, Charlie seemed to understand. "He's here, is he?" She nodded and he said, "We'd best let him know then." He pointed at the far side of the bay and she saw what looked like an army truck jolting along the rough coastal road. "More soldiers," Charlie said. "With a bit of luck, this lot will wait for them. Time enough, if we run."

He seized her hand and they ran off the causeway and up round the rock. The wind grabbed her hair. She panted, "How did you know?"

"Guessed. Niki said something. Hinted." He glanced at her. "Save your breath now."

Her legs thudded beneath her, jarring the bones of her face; her breath was sharp in her chest. She had never run so fast in her life; when they reached the gate of the town she thought she would die if she didn't stop for a minute. She staggered; lurched against Charlie. "My legs feel like jelly."

He tightened his grip on her hand. "Walk now, don't run. In case anyone notices, it'll look less suspicious."

She breathed deep and shudderingly. "What did Niki say?"

"Not much. It was what he didn't say, really. I asked him about Andreas Platonides, if he thought he might come back some day, and Niki said it was what they all prayed for. Then I told him we'd met Alexis and he looked sort of bothered. I said something like, poor kid, he must miss his father, and Niki shut up. Not just that—he went *cold* on me. I had a feeling—though of course I couldn't be sure. But I wasn't surprised when you told me."

There was only one person sitting outside the café when they reached the main square; an old man with his head sunk on his chest, dozing. The wind seemed less strong on this side of the rock, or perhaps it was slackening; as they went down the steps to Alexis's house, the sun flashed through a tear in the clouds.

Jo said, "He was supposed to leave last night in a boat but I should think the sea was too rough."

Charlie pulled a face. "He's lost his chance, then. He can't go now, not with that chopper about."

They were outside the door of the house. Jo saw Charlie's mouth twitch at the side as he tugged the bell. He stepped back and grinned at her nervously, wiping his hands on his jeans as if they were sweaty.

Hours seemed to pass. The heavy door opened a crack and Phoebe's fierce face peered suspiciously through it. Jo said, "Please, can we see Alexis?" Phoebe gabbled something, frowning with what looked like anger. Jo said, "It's *important*!" She thumped herself on the chest and jabbed with her forefinger. "*Me*. See *Alexis*!" The old woman shook her head and slammed the door in their faces.

They looked at each other. Charlie said, "Well, what now? If we can't make her understand and she won't let us in . . ."

"He may not be there, anyway."

"Can you think where he might be?"

She shook her head, sighing. Then said, "The bell! We could ring the old bell!" And, when Charlie looked blank, "Come on, I'll show you. Alexis told me it was used to warn people. If he hears it ringing he'll know . . ."

She didn't altogether believe this but it was a relief to have something to do. She led the way, racing up steps and through narrow alleys, Charlie panting behind her. As they reached the square he said, "Wait . . ." but she ran to the fig tree and set the bell swinging. The noise it made, a deep, solemn clanging, excited her. She pushed it again. "That's enough," Charlie said.

She stopped the bell with her hand but the echoes rolled richly on, round the rock, and birds flew out of nesting holes in the cliff and wheeled crying above them.

Charlie said, "We mustn't stay here." Jo looked at him, surprised by his tone, and saw he had gone deathly white. He said, urgently, "We'd better get back to the café. If there are any tourists about they'll be there, and we'll be safest with them."

Jo said, "What are you scared of? No one will hurt us, why should they? I'm going to stay here and wait for Alexis. Don't you see, it's my fault what's happened."

"You're not staying here."

"Yes, I am!"

"No, you're not. You're younger than I am, you'll do what I tell you." He got hold of her roughly and pushed her in front of him. He said, "For God's sake! They didn't send soldiers here to play *games*!"

His fear impressed her. She followed him meekly back to the main square and saw he was right to be frightened. This part of the town was alive with soldiers, running up side streets, kicking open the doors of the houses and shouting. An old woman with a cart load of fodder was leading her donkey into the square and a group of soldiers surrounded her. They jabbed their rifles into her pitiful bundles of greenery and then tipped the cart up. The old woman screamed wildly and the girl, Elena, ran out from the café and put an arm round her. One of the soldiers pulled Elena's long hair, jerking her head back, and kissed her. She spat in his face like an angry cat and led the old woman back to the café.

The soldiers laughed loudly. The old man who had been dozing at one of the tables stood up and waved his stick at them, but none of the other men who were gathered in the square now, said or did anything. They stood and watched sullenly while the soldiers searched the houses close by and then began climbing higher until the narrow streets of the town that had always seemed so quiet and deserted swarmed with yelling women, barking dogs, wailing children. Jo clung to Charlie. He said, "They won't interfere with us. At least, I don't think so. Just try and act ordinary."

They sat at the café and Elena came out for their order. She was pale but she smiled at them. She said, in halting English, "Do not be afraid of the soldiers." Her lip curled. "They are just rabble."

"Do you know why they're here?" Charlie asked and she shrugged and shook her head as if she didn't understand him. She brought their drinks and when she had gone, he looked at Jo curiously. "What did you mean when you said it was your fault?"

She stared at her lemonade. An insect had fallen in and was trying to swim, frail, cottony legs agitating the bubbles.

Charlie said, "You must have meant something."

She told him. She couldn't meet his eyes. She fished the insect out of her glass and let it dry on her finger.

After a little while, Charlie said, "You ought to have your mind seen to. If you really thought Alice . . ." He thumped his fist on the table. "Why didn't you say? If you couldn't think what to do, you should have asked Albert. Or me. Why on earth didn't you?"

"I don't know." It was the truth. She thought she had never felt so stupid and miserable.

Charlie said, softly and viciously, "You realise you may have spoiled everything? If there *was* a plan to overthrow the Dictator, you've probably ruined it. You and that idiot Alexis between you."

"You said he was lying!"

"Only because I didn't see how he could really know anything. I didn't know his father was here pretending to be a bald German, did I?" He laughed incredulously. "You know, I still can't believe it! I mean, you read these things in the *papers* . . ."

A familiar voice said, "This is terrible. Terrible."

Miss Emmeline and Miss Ottoline Skinner stood by their table. They both looked hot and dusty and Miss Emmeline's face was stiff with outrage. She said, "A disgrace to a civilised country! If I had not seen with my own eyes I would not have believed it. Those bullies! Bursting into people's houses, frightening women and children!"

"That is what bullies do," Miss Ottoline said. She seemed calmer than her cousin. She even smiled at Jo and Charlie as she sat down beside them. She put a camera on the table and touched it lovingly. "At least I have a record here!"

Charlie said, "You mean you've been taking pictures!" He sounded astonished.

"One should always be ready," Miss Ottoline said. "Some of these photographs will make an interesting contrast with those I took earlier. The peaceful streets—then the chaos of Armed Invasion. I got one excellent shot of a soldier breaking open a door with the butt of his rifle."

"You ought to be careful," Charlie said, reddening slightly. "I mean, if the soldiers saw you . . ."

Miss Ottoline giggled—an odd, girlish sound. "One of them did. He saw me and shouted. It was then that discretion seemed the better part of valour and I decided to retreat." She wagged her head merrily. "I must confess I was somewhat alarmed. He seemed very angry."

"There is no need for you to be afraid, Tilly," Miss Emmeline said. "We are American citizens. No one dare touch us!" She looked sternly at Jo and Charlie. "You two had better stay with us until the soldiers have gone. I cannot think they would do you any harm but I'm sure your parents would wish us to protect you. This is no place for children alone."

Charlie said, "Thank you, Miss Skinner."

He sounded as if he were trying not to laugh. Jo stared at him, wondering what he could find to laugh at, in this situation. She whispered, "I don't see what's funny."

"Don't you?" He glanced at Miss Emmeline Skinner and raised an eyebrow.

Miss Emmeline was on her feet. She said, "What's happening now, Tilly?"

The soldiers seemed to have finished their search and were drifting back to the square in small, ragged groups. From walls and windows and doorways the town's old women, like rows of perching, black crows, watched them in silence. Then, as more soldiers entered the square, in a compact, marching column, the silence was broken by a long, hushing sound, like a sigh, or waves breaking.

Miss Emmeline said in her strong, deep voice, "I think they have made an arrest."

At first they couldn't see the prisoner. Although he was tall for his age, the soldiers around him were taller. Then, as they drew near the cannon, old Phoebe, old Brown-Teeth, came running. She flung herself at one of the soldiers screeching and pummelling. He turned to push her hard in the face with the flat of his hand and they saw Alexis behind him. There was blood on his mouth and his shirt was torn but he held his head high.

From the door of the café, Elena said softly, "The boy. They have taken the boy . . ."

Miss Emmeline gasped. She said, "Tilly, this is an outrage. Do you see? They have arrested a child!"

Miss Ottoline seized her camera and leapt to her feet. Charlie said frantically, "Stop, don't do that," but he was too late. The soldiers were staring in Miss Ottoline's direction. Someone shouted something, an order, and two of them came swiftly towards her. One of them grabbed the camera, the other twisted her arm roughly behind her. Miss Ottoline screamed. Miss Emmeline cried, "Brute. Oh, you brute!" and advanced to the rescue, a small, stout, formidable figure, swinging her handbag. A tall officer slipped smoothly into her path and said, "It is forbidden to take photographs."

Miss Emmeline jutted her jaw. "Are you in charge here? If you are, I demand that you order your men to release this lady immediately. How dare you lay hands on her? We are visitors to this country. American citizens."

The officer said, "Visitors must also obey the law. It is not allowed to take pictures of a military operation. I regret, but we must take your friend to the police post. There will be an investigation."

Miss Ottoline wailed, "Emmy, my camera . . ."

The officer glanced at her, over his shoulder, and turned back to Miss Emmeline. "Your friend need not fear for her property. If all is in order it will be returned to her."

Miss Emmeline said, "I must warn you that you are making a grave mistake. I am a journalist and when I go home I will write about this in my paper. It will be very bad publicity for your country."

Charlie said, into Jo's ear, "Oh, the fool . . ." From the moment they first saw Alexis he had been holding her tightly.

Miss Emmeline stood very straight. Her colour had risen but she looked very dignified. She said, "If you are arresting my cousin, I insist that you arrest me as well."

"You may accompany us, certainly," the officer said.

He made a sign with his hand and the soldiers marched away with their prisoners. Miss Ottoline's head could be seen, craning round on her long neck as she was led from the square, but Alexis was lost in the midst of them.

Chapter 10

They climbed up, out of the Lower Town, to the Church of Santa Sophia. "Out of the way where no one will notice us," Charlie said. "Once they've started arresting foreigners you don't know where they will stop. Someone might tell them you know Alexis. They might want to question you."

He looked pale and shaken. Sitting on the parapet overlooking the sheer drop to the sea, Jo started to cry. She cried for relief, for escape, because Charlie was frightened. She moaned,"Oh, I wish Albert was here."

"Well, he isn't. And he couldn't do anything, anyway. Do shut up, Jo."

"I feel dreadful."

"No wonder, howling like that."

"What will they do to Alexis?"

"Make him talk," Charlie said grimly. "Tell them where his father is. If he didn't get off the rock last night, and I don't think he could have done, he must still be here, mustn't he? Not in his house, or anywhere in the town, because they'd have found him, but somewhere . . ."

Jo looked up at the ruined city, at the huge pink and grey stones stretching like a graveyard above them. Dark clouds raced over the sky and the top of the rock seemed to be moving.

Although there was no one to hear she felt she should whisper. "Up in the Citadel?"

"Perhaps. He could hide up there for ages. They'd need an army to find him, not just a few soldiers. I should think that's why they've arrested Alexis. To save them the trouble. If his father's so dotty about him he'll be bound to give himself up. He won't hide away safe while they torture his precious son."

She said, horrified, "They wouldn't torture him, Charlie! He's only a boy."

"Almost fourteen," Charlie said. "Not a *child.*"

"Don't," Jo said. "Don't . . ." She looked down the dizzy drop to the sea and thought of what Albert had said. *All those who died here.* Women and old men and children throwing themselves from this place rather than face the cruel enemy. She said, "I can't bear it."

"Don't think about it, then." Charlie gave a forced laugh, meant to cheer her. "Perhaps Miss Emmeline Skinner will stop them. I should think they'll have their hands full with her for a while. Those two women must be quite mad! Taking pictures of soldiers and boasting about writing articles for the newspapers when they get back to America. After all Albert has told them about what goes on in this country you'd have thought they'd know better."

Jo said, "Albert smuggled letters in. He could have been arrested for that. If they found out, he still might be."

"How do you know?"

"I was with him when he handed them over. That first

night in Zenith." She looked at him slyly. "When you were being so horrid."

He chose to ignore that. He whistled through his teeth and said, "Good old Albert!"

She would have laughed at him then but a new thought distracted her. "If Mr Platonides managed to hide from the soldiers why didn't Alexis go with him?"

"Perhaps he did. Perhaps his father sent him to see what was going on." He looked at Jo. "Or Alexis wanted to find out for himself. If he heard that old bell."

"Oh, Charlie!" She shivered and hugged herself. "I feel so cold . . ."

"It is cold." Charlie licked his finger and held it up. "Wind off the sea and starting to rain. We'd better go inside the Church. At least we'll be dry there."

It was dark inside the Santa Sophia. Most of the candles on the round metal stand were burnt out; only one flickered low. Jo dropped a coin in the box and took a new candle and lit it. Warm wax fell on her wrist as she fitted it into the holder.

Charlie said, "What's that for?"

"I don't know. Yes, I do!" She looked up at the painting of the kind Christ above her, at the gentle eyes and the hand lifted in blessing. She said, into the hollow quiet of the dome, "For Alexis. Keep him safe. Don't let them hurt him."

Charlie said, "That won't help, dummy."

"You can't tell."

"No." He laughed awkwardly. "I suppose it's worth trying."

She said, "How will his father know the soldiers have taken him?"

He didn't answer. He was standing at the door of the Church, looking out. He hissed, "Someone's coming. You'd better hide."

"Where?" Fear rose in her throat. She looked at the back of the Church, at the tattered red curtain that concealed the priest's hole. Would she be safe there? She started towards it, then thought she saw the curtain move. Was it the wind? She said, "Charlie . . ."

He shouted from the doorway. "It's all right, Jo! It's Albert!"

They raced to meet him by the flat tree. He was puffing and panting. He laughed when he saw them and pushed his glasses up on his nose. He said, "There you are, then! We met the Army truck on the road and turned back. We've been looking for you."

Charlie said, "I thought we'd be safer here. All those soldiers . . ." He rolled his eyes and staggered about drunkenly, acting out his relief. He said, in a comic voice, "Man, am I glad to see you!"

Jo said, "Albert. Oh, Albert," and he put his arms round her. He held her so tight she could hear his heart banging. She said, "Oh Albert, it's terrible. Poor Alexis! You've got to do something, quick!"

Albert said, "There's nothing anyone can do. Only wait."

Carrie's eyes glinted green. "There must be something! We could go and protest. About the American women, anyway! They can't keep them there, at the police station."

"Oh yes they can," Albert said.

They ate lunch inside the restaurant of the hotel, watching the grey rain stream down the windows. Grey rain and grey sea and grey clouds drifting pale fingers down the side of the rock. After they had eaten the rain stopped and the wind backed and changed. They sat on the terrace watching the sky clear; clouds rolling back before the brisk breeze. Sun danced on the sea, hard and bright, and white gulls swooped over it. Alice said, "It's nice now. Can James and me go and look at the helicopter? We're getting bored, doing nothing."

"If you look after James," Albert said. "And don't go too close."

"I'll go with them," Jo offered but he shook his head. He smiled at her but his eyes were not laughing. His expression made her heart flutter. She said, "I'm not scared of the soldiers. Do you think they'd arrest me? That would be exciting." She rocked her chair backwards and forwards and giggled.

"Don't act the fool," Charlie said.

Carrie laughed, "Sometimes it helps. Don't be sharp, Charlie."

Albert said, "We don't know what Alexis has told them.

Or Alice's policeman. Or what they suspect. If they're just holding the boy as a bait for his father that's one thing. If they have any suspicion that there's something more going on . . ." He looked at Jo and lowered his voice. ". . . something on the lines of that colourful story Alexis has told you, then that's something else. Something dangerous. If they should take it into their heads to ask you some questions, then your mother and I must be with you."

Your mother and I. It had a heavy, solemn ring that alarmed and embarrassed her. She took refuge in childishness—and knew she was doing it. She wriggled and pouted. "Oh, all right, then. But I feel just like Alice! I'm getting bored, waiting!"

The sun moved across the blue sky and the great rock began to turn pink in the afternoon light. At about tea time—or what would have been tea time on a normal day—Miss Emmeline Skinner returned from the police post. She had been arguing and complaining for several hours and it had given her an excellent appetite. She attacked the meal Niki gave her with gusto, talking between mouthfuls and stabbing the air with her fork to make points. "They won't get away with it," she said, with a snort. "As I told that young officer in the very beginning. Not that the Army is in charge of this operation, of course. As soon as I realised that, I insisted on seeing the person responsible. It took time but I made it clear I had plenty of *that*, no other pressing engagements, and I was finally ushered into the Presence. A mean-looking fat man in a dark suit and dark glasses. Secret Police, I said to myself as soon as I saw him. They wear the same uniform all the world over! Oh, he was polite enough to begin with. He even apologised for keeping me waiting. I told him it was my cousin he was keeping waiting, not me, and he said that was a question of National Security but he was sure, once his men had completed their investigations, everything would turn out quite in order. It had better be, I told him, or you'll be in trouble when our Ambassador hears what you've done with poor Tilly." She waved her fork wildly and bits of food flew about. "As he shall hear, just as soon as young Niki can get a call through to our Embassy."

"The telephone's out of order," Albert said. "I've already tried to ring Zenith. Did you find out what had happened to the boy?"

"I enquired, naturally. I asked what he was charged with. The man affected not to understand me."

"I doubt if they've charged him with anything," Albert said. "They're just holding him. It's a political matter."

"So I understood in the end. I told the policeman—in my country, we don't arrest the children of our political opponents. It was then that he had me thrown out. Well, not thrown, exactly. Pushed. I was pushed. A soldier assisted me, you might say, from the room. "She took a mouthful of meat and chewed thoughtfully. "In a way, I'm not sorry that this has happened. I've been given a chance to see for myself how this country is run, and I'm grateful for that. Otherwise I might have gone home with a quite false impression. To be honest, I had begun to think some of the things I had heard were exaggerated. Even some of the things, Mr Sandwich, that you had told me." She thrust out her chin. "I must tell you that I'm ashamed to have doubted you. I don't now."

"Thank you," Albert said. "Though I wish, for your cousin's sake, you hadn't had to find out the truth so uncomfortably."

She looked at him. "Are you laughing at me? Maybe you're right to. I must look like an ignorant old woman to you. Even, perhaps, rather comic."

"Not at all," Albert said. "I think you've been brave. Not everyone would have been quite so ready to tackle the Secret Police."

Miss Emmeline wiped her plate clean with a piece of bread and put her knife and fork neatly together like a good child. She said sadly, "I fear it was simply a matter of fools rushing in where angels fear to tread."

"At least you've done something," Carrie said.

Miss Emmeline sighed. "One small thing, anyway. I was allowed to see Tilly for a couple of minutes. She was in excellent spirits—she is very couragoeus—and she said she was perfectly well, only anxious about her camera, and hungry. It hardly seemed tactful to mention the camera to anyone, but I was able to speak to our nice young policeman and he promised to get some food for her and the boy."

Jo said, "Alice's policeman?"

"The one from the village. A pleasant young man with an agreeable smile and a fondness for lilies." Miss Emmeline beamed. "The unaffected way the men here walk about with flowers in their hands is really quite charming."

Jo said, "That first evening, when Alice . . ." She caught her breath. "*Albert*! Do you remember? Herr Schmidt came to the café. He talked to us, then he sat down with the policeman. You'd have thought he'd be scared!"

"Bluff," Albert said. "It made him look innocent, didn't it? An innocent tourist. Maybe Andreas enjoys a bit of fun, too." He looked at Carrie. "Like that performance when the cruise ship came in. He got into his stride then, didn't he? Herr Schmidt from Hamburg acting his character part." He laughed softly. "Over-acting, I thought."

Carrie said, "You might have told me you knew who he was. Albert Spy-Boots! I thought you were being so feeble!"

"Sorry, love. But it wasn't my secret."

They smiled at each other. Jo saw that they had both forgotten how she had behaved on that occasion, how she had called Albert a traitor and run off in tears. It made her feel strange as if something important, some focus, had shifted. They had forgotten it because it wasn't important to them. *She* wasn't as important to them as they were to each other! It made her feel lonely and sad for a minute, and then Charlie winked at her and she knew he remembered. She grinned and winked back.

"Herr Schmidt?" Miss Emmeline said. "Do you mean *our* Herr Schmidt?"

"Our Herr Schmidt is Andreas Platonides," Albert said. "The boy's father. He came into the country on a false passport. It was the only way he could visit his son."

"Gracious goodness," Miss Emmeline said. For a moment, she digested this information in silence. Then she said, "How extraordinary," in a tone that meant, "How exciting." She went on, rather wistfully, "To think I had no idea! I've always heard of Mr Platonides as a fine man, a true statesman. He once came to New York to speak at the United Nations and the man who covered his speech for our paper said it was a fine, inspiring performance. I do wish I'd known who he was! I would have been very discreet but I would have liked—just once—to have shaken his hand. Tilly will feel the same way when she knows. It would have been a really wonderful thing if she could have taken his picture. A wonderful story!" Her deep voice shook with emotion. "At least it will be a wonderful memory for the rest of our lives! One to treasure! To think we have stayed under the same roof as such a great Fighter for Freedom! It's like finding oneself part of history."

She took out her handkerchief and blew her nose loudly.

Albert said gently, "Unfortunately, it's not a memory yet. We're still in the middle of it."

Miss Emmeline mopped her eyes. She put her handkerchief away and bowed her head. She said, "Please forgive me. I was carried away." She looked up at Albert. "That poor little boy. Surely they will let him go soon?"

"When they get what they want," Albert said.

Jo burst out, "Alexis isn't a little boy! He wouldn't want his father to give himself up! Whatever they do to him . . ."

She thought of the things they could do; horrible things she had read about. Would *she* be brave if they said to her, "Tell us, now, did your stepfather smuggle letters into this country?" If they threatened her? Her stomach shrank flat to her spine and her mouth went dry. She said, "Alexis is brave."

Charlie said in a loud voice, "There were some kidnappers once who cut a boy's ear off and sent it to his parents to make them pay some huge ransom. They sent the ear through the post." He laughed stupidly. "I think that was in Italy."

Albert said, "There will be no need for that." He swallowed and looked very white. "Andreas knows perfectly well what they can do to his son."

For a moment, no one spoke or moved. It was as if a kind of shame held them; the thought of what people could do to each other. Then Miss Emmeline rose from her seat at the table as if she wished to make an announcement. She said, in her deep voice, "There is only one cell in that jail. Tilly is locked up with the boy. They won't lay a finger on him while Tilly is there, I can promise you. That woman may appear gentle but she has the heart of a lion!"

Her kind eyes shone with heroic dreams. Jo saw her

bright, dreaming look and knew, with a sinking heart, that no old woman, even a brave one, could protect Alexis if the Secret Police wanted to harm him. She was surprised to hear Albert say, with a note of respect in his voice, "I hope you're right. In fact, I think you may well be."

As they walked to the village to collect James and Alice, Jo said, "Did you mean that, Albert? Or were you cheering us up?"

"Partly, perhaps," Albert said. "But there's a fair chance that Miss Ottoline may stop them behaving too badly. The Dictator is sensitive to foreign opinion—Ithaca gets a lot of American aid, for one thing—and the police will have seen enough of the Skinners by now to know they're unlikely to keep quiet once they're home."

Charlie chuckled. "Miss Emmeline would get on to the President."

"Oh, at least," Albert said.

They passed the police post, a small, white-washed building on the edge of the village. Lilies and roses grew in neat beds around it and a climbing shrub framed the doorway with blue, bell-like flowers. Several soldiers lounged on a bench outside, smoking and talking; others sat at the harbour café. Jo held Carrie's hand tight. She whispered, "Nothing seems to be happening."

Apart from the soldiers, and the helicopter on the causeway, the mainland village looked much as usual. Shops and cafés were open, gulls cried round the rock and wheeled over the boats rocking at anchor; on the jetty, old men with brown, weathered faces sat and dozed in the sun.

Alice and James came running, their mouths smeared and sticky. James said, "Alice's policeman bought us both an ice-cream. I had vanilla and Alice had strawberry."

"You'd think he'd be ashamed," Charlie said, and Alice looked at him blankly.

She said indignantly, "Someone threw a stone at the policeman. Some horrid, rude boy. I chased him and hit him."

Albert looked at Charlie and laughed. Charlie pulled a face back. Alice looked from one to the other and said, "What's the matter?"

Carrie said quickly, "Nothing, my darling. You're a brave girl to stick up for your friend. Would you like to go swimming? It's warm enough now and the sea's a lot calmer."

They went back to the hotel and changed. It seemed odd to Jo to be doing something so ordinary; putting on her bathing suit, walking over the rocks to the sea, stopping on the way to look in a pool, scraping at a patch of dried salt with her finger nail. The odd feeling persisted after she had dived in the water. It was warm and silky to touch and the evening sun turned it pink and golden and black. Jo swam in this coloured sea and remembered a picture she had seen once of people at a fair, all of them busy, all doing different things in their own corners and taking no notice of what went on around them. She picked up a handful of sea and let it fall in sparkly drops from her fingers and thought the whole world was like that. Even when terrible things were happening, people fighting or dying or being locked up in prison, everyone else went calmly on with what they were doing; eating or playing or sleeping or swimming. She lay on her back and tried to think of Alexis. She made a picture in her mind—Alexis, sitting in a small room with Miss Ottoline Skinner and a sinister man in dark glasses peering through a grille at them—but it wouldn't stay fixed. It faded and slipped away and all she could see was herself, drifting lazily on the surface of the warm sea with her hair floating like seaweed about her.

She heard Charlie shout. She flipped her legs down, treading water, and saw the helicopter take off from the causeway, red dust whirling behind it. It rose in the air like some huge, ancient insect, dipped briefly over the sea, then turned and clattered off round the rock. When it had gone and the last echoes died, a donkey started to bray on the mainland; a sad, harsh, lonely honking.

She looked at the shore. Charlie was hauling himself up on the rocks. He turned and waved, beckoning her in with an urgent wave of his arm, then ran, clumsily stumbling, towards the hotel. Miss Emmeline Skinner was out on her balcony, wearing a bright floral wrapper, and Carrie and Albert were on the concrete below her. They were all looking towards the village and the great rock that rose above it, dark red in the last of the sun, the colour of old bricks, or blood.

Jo swam as fast as she could. Her legs were trembly and

weak; when she reached land they buckled beneath her and she stumbled as Charlie had done. She slipped and went down, cutting her hands, but felt nothing. She scrambled up and ran on, holding her bleeding hands out in front of her. Her head was light and empty and singing. She thought she would fall again, faint, but she kept on somehow and got to Albert and Carrie just as Niki came roaring up on his motor scooter to tell them the long wait was over. While they had been peacefully swimming, Andreas Platonides had come down from the Citadel and given himself up to the police.

He came down at sunset. He had shaved off his beard and as he walked proudly through the streets of the town the people recognised him and fell silent. If he had made one sign, said one word, they would have fought for him, bare hands against bayonets, but Andreas Platonides looked neither to right nor to left. He must have wrestled with demons, up there on the cold, lonely rock, but his pale handsome face was quite calm. He had made his decision and came to rescue his son. Although he was his people's hope, their beloved leader, he was a father first and foremost.

This was part of the article Miss Emmeline wrote when she got back to America. There were no illustrations because when the police set Miss Ottoline free they confiscated her film, but Albert said Miss Emmeline's passionate prose made pictures unnecessary.

"That'll teach you not to believe all you read in the papers," he said when he showed us the cutting Miss Emmeline sent him. He meant she had written as if she had seen it all for herself. I knew she hadn't because she was on her balcony when Niki came to tell us what happened—how the soldiers had seized Andreas Platonides at the gate of the town and hustled him into the helicopter with a sack over his head— but when I read her story again it seemed to me that this was how it must have been, and I knew it was how I would always see it in my mind.

Albert laughed when I told him this. "Writers are powerful people, Jo. That's why you must always try and write the truth. As near as you can get to it, anyway."

I have tried to do that. I have written what happened as it seemed to me at the time, although of course I understand more, now that I'm older. I know that brave men can act stupidly and that great events often turn on small things. Andreas Platonides did a stupid thing, coming to Polis where everyone knew him so well. He should have known there was a risk someone might give him away, perhaps without meaning to. As Alice and I did between us. And stopped a revolution . . .

Alexis was telling the truth. That was another stupid thing Andreas Platonides did—trusting a boy with such a dangerous secret. It was lucky for him (and for Alexis) that the Secret Police never guessed there was more to his visit than a father's wish to see his only son. Andreas was taken to Zenith and put under house arrest but nothing worse happened to him and the secret was kept.

All that is history now. In the history books. The Dictator fell eighteen months later, overthrown by the same Generals who had put him in power. He had grown old and ill and they turned on him, Albert said, like a pack of wolves will turn on a leader when he loses his strength and cunning. The Generals ruled for another year, then they held free elections and Andreas Platonides became the Prime Minister. A book was published about the Dictator called *The Rise and Fall of a Tyrant*, and on page 274 there is a paragraph about the naval rebellion that was planned for the National Day but which never took place because Andreas Platonides was arrested in his home town of Polis. Nothing about me, of course, and I am grateful for that because whenever I thought about it I felt breathless and screwed up inside.

I still do, though less than I used to. Albert says we all have to learn from the past and education is seldom painless. He says revolutions can be good sometimes even if people die, because not to be free is a kind of death, too. But if this revolution had gone ahead, at a time when the Dictator was still fit and powerful and had the Army behind him, it might have been very bloody. Some of the people who would have died might have been people we knew. Niki, perhaps. Or, on the other side, Alice's policeman. "I doubt if he would have left Polis alive," Albert says. "Too many people had old scores to settle."

Albert says, Albert says . . . I don't pay as much attention to him as I used to, not as much as Charlie does now, but I always listen when he talks about Ithaca. Everyone has a special place, one to visit in dreams, and that great, lonely rock and the small secret town huddled beneath it is Albert's and mine.

"Would you like to go back?" he said yesterday. "Nothing to stop us, now things are more settled. We could go, this summer."

James and Alice and Charlie all started jabbering but I was too full to speak. Albert said, "Jo, you're quiet," and I knew from the smile in his eyes that he understood why.

I nodded—it was all I could manage—and he said, "You'd better write to Alexis and tell him.

I found my tongue then. "Oh, I *can't*." There were so many reasons. I picked one. "He's not written to me."

Albert looked at Carrie and they both burst out laughing.

I said angrily, "It's not funny! He might not want to see me!"

Albert took off his glasses and wiped his eyes. He said, "There's only one way to find out. You're not too proud, are you? It's usually a mistake not to write." He put his glasses back on and looked at Carrie again, tender and smiling, and I stopped being angry because I could see they hadn't been laughing at me but at something private between them.

Alice said, "Will my policeman be there?"

Charlie groaned and rolled his eyes upwards.

Alice said, "I want him to be! I want everything to be just the same!" She clenched her fists and shook.

"It won't be," Albert said. "Nothing ever is. Nothing stays still. You're different, Alice. You're older and taller."

He spoke to her but he was telling me something, too. He looked at me very straight, not smiling at all, and said, "There's always a risk, going back. It's up to you, Jo. Do you want to?"

They all looked at me, quiet and waiting. Charlie as tall as Albert now; Alice grown leggy and even more beautiful; James so much fatter and sturdier. I felt a lot of things jumbled together; excited and scared and happy and sad. Excited at the thought of moving on, growing older, and sad at the thought of time passing. I said, "Of course I want to go, don't be silly," and went upstairs to my room to start writing my letter.